DEATH
AT A FESTIVAL

JUDE AND ALISON ALEXANDER

EER FICTION
Edward Everett Root, Publishers Co. Ltd.
Atlas Chambers, 33 West Street, Brighton, BN1 2RE, England

Full details of our stock-holding overseas agents in America,
Australia, China, Europe, Japan, and North America, and
how to order our books, are given on our website. *We stand
with Ukraine. EER books are not for sale in Belarus or Russia.*

www.eerpublishing.com
edwardeverettroot@yahoo.co.uk

Death at a Festival
© Jude & Alison Alexander 2024

First published in England by Edward Everett Root
Publishers, 2024. This edition © Edward Everett Root
Publishers 2024.

ISBN 9781915115416 hardback
ISBN 9781915115423 paperback

Cover design and book production by Julie Hawkins

THURSDAY

Mother

I've never seen so many penises in all my life. I'm gawping like an idiot, trying to close my mouth — but it keeps dropping again in astonishment. I'm at a hippie festival. It's like nothing I've ever seen, never in all my born days. My dear daughter Chris has brought me here. She thinks I'll love it.

Chris adores HipHaven. She's been going for years, and she's been asking me to come for years, too. I've politely declined, saying I'm too old to get up from the floor in a tent, but this year she rang with a new message. 'If I give you a real bed off the ground, will you come to HipHaven?' So here I am. All mothers will know why. Fathers, sisters and brothers won't. I notice this when I tell people where I'm going.

HipHaven is held in the remote backblocks of New South Wales, five hours from Melbourne and many more from Sydney and Adelaide. Twice a year, four or five thousand people congregate on a huge circle of land by a river. I read the blurb sent out by the organisers: vegetarian, clothing optional, no naked flames or amplified music. And because it's out of range and there's no electricity, there aren't any phones, ipads, computers or any sort of electronic gadgets. All noise is made by humans, or birds, on the spot. It's like being back in the 1970s, or even the 1950s, not because of the hippies but because of the absence of anything electronic or even electric. And Chris tells me you're not allowed to take photos, unless you ask permission from everyone in them. That pretty well stops any photography, so no cameras or ipads or anything are used at all. No gadgets. Nothing beeping at you.

It starts when Chris picks me up in Melbourne, where I'm staying with my other daughter, Laura. She lives in inner-city Carlton, and loves having coffee in cafes, dining at interesting restaurants and sipping delicious cocktails. She's an enthusiastic green with a caustic wit, and no hippie. She's horrified that I'm going to HipHaven, which she wouldn't attend in a million years, and she's so convinced I'll be uncomfortable and miserable that, just in case, she kindly gives me a key to her house, as a refuge if I can't bear it and leave early. She and her partner are going camping: civilised camping. When I visit my daughters in Melbourne, I have to take two separate outfits and mentalities. They get on pretty well, in a slightly bemused way.

Chris and I drive out of Melbourne and into the country, going north. Over the hills and into country that is flat, flatter, flattest. The vegetation changes from lush in the hills to drier eucalypt country. Soon we're driving through towns I've never heard of. We stop for the night at Echuca on the Murray, a pretty town where we have a wonderful sophisticated dinner at an Asian restaurant, sitting outside under the stars — Echuca doesn't even have mosquitoes. When I was a girl, towns like Echuca wouldn't have known sophisticated Asian restaurants existed. Hobart, where I grew up, was just the same. Now there's been a revolution. Thank goodness.

Next day we have traditional bacon and eggs for breakfast — cooked just right and quite as delicious as last night's. Seeing a second-hand bookshop open and remembering that my ipad won't work at the festival, I buy five Agatha Christies. We drive on, through Deniliquin, across the Murray, into New South Wales and on for another hour. We're into the flattest country here. Not so much as a hillock, right to the horizon. It's all red soil and grey-brown vegetation. Chris knows the trees: Murray pines, eucalypts, saltbush. It's marginal country for farming, she says, dry and not very fertile. Farmers grow any crop they can, including rice. Rice! Why rice, that needs so much water? She shrugs. Farmers do it tough: if there's a space in the market, they fill it. We wonder about the pioneers, stuck out here hours from anywhere on horseback, no refrigeration, nothing except what they can grow and make. I'm wondering why HipHaven is held here, so far from anywhere. I forget to ask Chris. Cheap land? Away from it all? So far that only devotees attend, weeding out the fainthearts who might not take it seriously, just go for the drugs?

I can sense Chris getting more alert, excited: HipHaven is near. 'We can start to look for HipHaven cars', she says. I peer about, expecting the flower power vans of my youth. The road is disappointingly empty, and the few cars we see are respectable modern ones, some piled with baggage (HipHaven), others dusty and driven fast (locals). Not a flower in sight.

Chris recognises landmarks. We're almost there! Willy nilly I can feel myself becoming, if not excited, at least anticipatory. What's it going to be like? Here's the turn-off! A group of people are waving us to turn. We drive along a dusty, bumpy dirt road and up to the entrance. We're here!

Usually at big events — say, a footy game in Melbourne — you're checked in by a security guard in uniform and a hi-vis vest. Not at HipHaven. Here we're welcomed, really welcomed not just have-a-nice-dayed, by a man in harem pants playing a recorder. He's a cheerful faun, who checks our tickets and waves us forward. Chris is bubbling over, recognising people, waving, being waved to: it's all impressively positive and warm. There's a sign: 'Welcome to HipHaven. Please adjust your clocks to your constellation time.' I feel like groaning, but smile weakly to appear enthusiastic. Does constellation time exist? I certainly don't know mine.

We find a park among the thousands of cars, pick up our tents and walk to the entrance. The car park is at the north of HipHaven's circle of land. The rest is for camping under gum trees, with blocks of long drop bush toilets scattered around. In the centre are communal activities: mud bath, hot spa, paint tent, hug pit, cuddle puddle, permaculture people and so on. I hope the 'so on' includes showers. There's also a huge performance area, ringed by market stalls (clothes, jewellery, food). Everything is connected by dirt paths.

The entrance is a large gate with a headdress of red flags, like tongues of flame. The entrance to Hell? Surely not, at this peace-loving event. I mean to ask Chris, but the sight that meets my eyes — fortunately behind sunglasses, so my eyes starting out of my head aren't obvious — sends any such thoughts right out of my mind.

Clothing is certainly optional. People wear all sorts of garments except ordinary ones (and I use 'ordinary' in the sense of 'used by the majority', of course, not being judgmental in any way). Men in satin ball gowns or tutus; women in diaphanous skirts; men in man kilts, dashing little skirts which Chris tells me are all the rage; a man in full Native American feather headdress — but Chris frowns at that. Cultural misappropriation. I can cope with that (I hadn't heard the term before, but it is cultural misappropriation, of course, if you think about it), but what does startle me is the nudity, naked people walking along quite unconcernedly, breasts or penises bobbing away. Breasts I'm used to, but the penises! So many different shapes and sizes. A little knobbly one, dwarfed by the balls behind it. Long thin pink ones, dangly, like thin sausages. Short fat ones, almost square. Jaunty ones, bobbing from side to side. A huge, extended one, with throbbing veins: I wince. Big, small, thin, fat, short, long, they're all around me. And because most of these HipHaven attendees are young and firm, their bodies look wonderful. Like artists' models. It becomes normal in about five minutes — in a world where nothing is normal.

The older ones aren't so wonderful, though. Here comes a woman, perhaps in her fifties, wearing a frumpy floral cotton shirt and nothing else. She has an enormous bush of dark frizzy pubic hair and a large and dimpled bum. And she's walking along the path quite unconcerned. Great not to bother about your appearance, of course, but ... not quite like the young ones.

What on earth have I done, I wonder, trudging along beside Chris, carrying my tent, fully clothed and intending to remain so. Coming here with four thousand other people, for five whole days, to camp and be uncomfortable in the middle of a mass of people in the nude, just because Chris likes it. The things you do for your children. Watching hockey in the freezing cold on Saturday mornings, picking them up from inconvenient places at inconvenient times, listening to their sorrows at length ... But nothing else has been like this. I don't know a soul here beside Chris, and at the moment I don't want to. I could be at home in my comfortable chair with a cup of tea, reading a book, looking up my emails, chatting to a friend on the phone, doing some work. Work looks really good at the moment. (I write historical books.)

But here I am. I might as well make the best of it, I tell myself. No use grizzling, even inwardly. As Brown Owl used to say, 'A Brownie smiles and sings under all difficulties'. So I'm smiling and singing. Sort of.

We find a good campsite, shaded by the magnificent gum trees with their grey-white trunks. We erect our tents, a little one for Chris and a huge one for me, so big I can stand up inside it. Another bribe, along with the bed. Marvellous.

Then we trudge the kilometre back to the car for more of our stuff. It's hot. Hot, hot, hot. A bus is rumoured to take people and their luggage into the campsite, so we wait where people think it might stop, in the middle of a car park in a dusty plain stretching to the horizon, under a hard, blue, unremittingly cloudless sky. We're sweaty and smelly and we've run out of water. 'This is awful, Chris', I say. 'We'll never forget it. We'll remind each other of it for years and years. Everything else will be better.' Kids are whingeing: 'When will the bus come?' How good to be six, to think that just asking the question will make the bus appear, magicked up by all-powerful parents.

Well, it works, or something does. Here comes the bus, an old rattletrap with 'Kathmandu Express' painted on the side, surrounded by flowers, hippie-style. At last! Transport and the good old days, rolled into one! We all throw our stuff in the back and climb in. No seat belts. People standing everywhere. People leaning out the door. Kids sitting on the luggage. It doesn't matter. The bus is so slow, no one's going to be hurt. In the spirit of HipHaven we all start chatting to each other, discussing where the bus will stop, where we'll land if we fall over, whether we can squeeze up to make more room.

The bus stops somewhere near our campsite and we pile off, eventually finding ourselves standing with a mound of luggage in a central space. 'We need a trolley', says Chris. They're in demand. By now I'm used to nudity. I'd a good deal rather see a trolley than a penis. There's one — but someone else gets to it. A man points to another one, away under a tree. I race to it: no one's going to get between it and me. Fortunately for my peaceful behaviour at HipHaven, they don't. On goes the luggage and, miraculously, clever Chris finds our campsite. Soon she has the kettle on, making tea.

Opposite us a family sets up. Ominous. 'Nimrod, would you like to come here?' 'It might be better if you didn't do that, Onyx.' I feel sorry for the adults, their parenting so public. You can't be cross with anyone at HipHaven. Not out loud, anyway. The parents are admirably patient. 'If you didn't have a bike, wouldn't you like someone else to share with you? So take turns with Nimrod.' The children aren't so calm. They're playing Pig in the Middle, and one thinks he's been pig too long. 'I'm telling!' He storms off, but it all dies down.

We go to see what's happening. Down by the river is the place to be. There's a mud bath, a huge pool of viscous grey sludge with nude people wallowing in it. If you're really serious, you get out, roll in dirt, branches, twigs, leaves and so on, and wander round the camp looking like — well, I can't really think of anything. A sort of mobile scruffy bush. A lamington, says Laura when I tell her the story. Chris says people sometimes jibber in tongues, but sadly I don't see anyone doing this. I think she imagined I might like to join in. Poor darling.

I don't even go in the hot tub. They're having a women's hour. You strip off (if you're wearing anything to strip), rub yourself with a mixture of sugar and olive oil, then get in the tub — very hot, by the reaction of the devotees. Chris leaps at the chance, but I hang back (boringly, but it's hard to make yourself do something utterly foreign to the whole of your previous 66 years). She does the anointing, bringing me a bit of olive oil to try it out on my arms, then joins the throng in the hot tub. ('Hippie soup!' snorts Laura.) A woman leads the others in chanting. It sounds fantastic, really fantastic in the fantasy sense, echoing amid the gums from ecstatic faces. Along the riverbank, someone's playing the didgeridoo, someone else the guitar. It's like a painting by Streeton, eucalypts leering over the river banks, the greys, browns and greens. People are swimming, despite a warning that blue-green algae give you an itchy rash. That wasn't in Streeton's script, and people ignore it. I can feel myself relaxing. This isn't too bad. I can cope with this.

After a while Chris emerges from the hot tub, beautifully rosy pink. 'The Adelaidies!' She rushes up to a group of particularly cheerful women wearing fabulously coloured sarongs. They shout joyfully in recognition. There are big hugs, smooches, cries of joy. 'This is my Mum!' 'Wonderful! Hi, Mum!' The Adeladies come from Adelaide every year, and they're well in the running for the loveliest, happiest, most warmness-radiating people I've ever met. They've just finished the ten-hour trip, they're full of beans, they're here for a good time and, my goodness, they're having it.

This is my introduction to HipHaven. A lot of things impress me, mainly the wonderful, peaceful, harmonious atmosphere. Everyone is so thoroughly nice, so helpful. No pushing, no shoving. Queues for the long drop toilets: 'Who was first?' 'Weren't you here before me?' No rubbish dropped, no trace left. And the non-judgmental atmosphere, though a little challenging to maintain, means everyone can be themselves, wear anything, do anything, be entirely free. The setting sun shines down through the gum trees on a scene of tranquillity and harmony.

Daughter

What's great about Mum is she's genuinely interested in everything. I point out the changes of the land as we drive through — the chain of low hills they call the Great Dividing Range, carpeted with gums, to the relatively lush wine country around Harcourt, then north into the wheat belt, the start of the bare red earth and grey gums. We stay overnight at Echuca, between the sickly green Murray, still mighty and dotted with steamboats, to the emerald Campaspe.

We are both from Tasmania and though I've been gone twenty years, there is a conviction in my soul that wattles are silver, not gold, and waratahs should be small and red as rosebuds. And I miss the pink mountain berries and the purple hills and the clean smell of the bush and the bite to the wind that sweeps north from Antarctica.

But I believe that even Tasmanians should go once in their lives to the hard country of inland mainland Australia, where the bush bakes in the heat and smells like dust and sounds like a dry rustle in the wind. Where now and again on a hot summer's day, you hear a crash as a mighty branch lets go and falls to the ground without warning. You need to feel the nighttime peace and the million stars and the white trunks of the river red gums skirting the river.

The next morning, we drive north and then west, seeing the change to grey box and then the true hard country, black box and saltbush with now and again a twisted Murray pine or the green grace of a peppercorn tree. Out here the acacias are small and shrubby with a spray of tiny yellow flowers in season. The plains are saltbush and grass, and crows and kites fly overhead. This is where we camp, where the land is the colour of dry terracotta, among the gums, and the plains are the soft grey-green of the saltbush.

I describe it to Mum in the hope that she wouldn't see it as the back of beyond, like city people often do, as a nothing space we can rubbish and ignore. To me it is full of life and possibility and promise.

I needn't have doubted her. Mum is a lifelong bushwalker. 'Isn't this lovely,' she says. 'Look at these gums, aren't they pretty?' I watch her settle into her chair and open a book, calm and relaxed in the bush. I relax.

The rivers have carved deep trenches and are flowing sluggishly along the bottoms. They still have no vegetation to stabilise their banks and the paddocks they flow through are painfully bare. And topsoil there once was is gone. I used to date a farmer, and one day we sat down and listed all the farming innovations brought out from England that failed in Australia. We filled an A4 sheet in ten minutes. The mouldboard plough. Foxes. Now the upstream fertilisers have washed into the Murray system and helped breed massive amounts of green algae, and the river is once again toxic. So we can't swim, and cattle are at risk when they drink the water, and the 90 per cent of Australians who live in the cities don't care at all until it affects them. And they vote, and they decide where the money goes. The rivers are our veins, the land our body.

Yearly, the European carp move further up the river system, nibbling the banks away and turning hundreds of kilometres of the river brown. In living memory, you could see the bottom of the Murray. Now if you dive under, you can't see your hand in front of your face.

How to camp

Or more properly, how *I* camp. Anyone can camp, it's a matter of assembling the main nine things, driving somewhere in the bush, disassembling the things and staying there. From then on, it's a process of refinement. If you set up in the evening, you realise in the morning that the sun is baking your tent and you wish you'd put it in the shade of that tree. Or you didn't sleep well because you are on a slope and wish you'd set up on a flat spot.

When you have camped many times, you become so bogged down with these considerations that looking for a spot to put the tent involves standing quite still in the bush, slowly revolving and staring, slackjawed, into the middle distance. People you have taken camping for the first time think you have become slightly unhinged and are doing nothing and they tend to interrupt (where do you want to go? Shall we go over here? Argh what are we doing and spiders and snakes and couldn't we have booked a B and B?), but thankfully my mum isn't one of those people and seems to have worked out that a process is going on. Still, she says, 'what about over here?' and I say, 'no, there will be two hours of sun from one to three', and she says, 'that's OK', and I say, 'no, it's not'. And she leaves me to it.

The considerations, if you are interested, are:

Sun: rises just north of east and sets just north of west and tracks an arc just north of the top of the sky. The important shade times are morning (trees to the east) and midday (trees overhead and slightly north).

Slope: we need two flat spots for two tents, one very large.

Slope: if two inches of rain fall, where will it pool and will the tents be in it?

Neighbours: Look for and avoid young people with a lot of beer, babies and small children. They are the noisiest nighttime campers in any cohort, except for the most annoying neighbours of all: old people in caravans with generators. Luckily, those last can't get in here. Old people don't sleep as much and old men tend to get up early and put their generators on at 7am and the grey drone will go through your earplugs and fill your head with boredom and hate and wakefulness.

Death: avoid camping under large, and especially dead eucalyptus branches which could kill you if they fall on your tent. I aim for tiny leafy feathery branches that would bounce off the tent.

Fauna: avoid ant nests and snake holes. Also with snakes, avoid logpiles, which they tend to favour.

Spirit: I generally ask the bush where it wants me to camp, but I don't tell Mum this in case she thinks I'm bonkers.

Eventually, the bush leads me to a nice spot with two flat areas, feathery trees to the north and a neighbouring logpile. 'I think here is good', I say to Mum, and she agrees and we start unrolling the tents. I don't tell her about the snakes. They often hide when there are a lot of people around.

We are setting up when a baby starts to wail, loudly. I look at Mum and she looks at me. Oh well. No place is perfect.

Oh, and my nine main things are:

Keys, wallet, phone.

Tent, sleeping mat, sleeping bag.

Clothes, food, toiletries.

Mother

Chris and I have dinner at our campsite. First we have starters. She's brought everything I might like. Tins of dolmades, corn chips and tapenade, olives, gherkins. All good. Then we make dinner. That is, she does the hard work, cooking a tomato omelette on a small stove in cramped conditions, and I cut up a salad. Even this is a bit challenging, sitting in my folding chair (a third bribe) leaning over to chop on a board on the ground. But Nimrod's father is playing the violin behind us, and it all tastes delicious, eaten as the sun is setting, long golden rays slanting between the trees. We have a cup of tea and I wash up, rather scrappily from a lack of hot water, soap and light. Chris puts the dishes on a tree stump so they can have a bit of sun tomorrow. She says, optimistically, that sunshine kills germs. Let's hope something does.

Daughter

Once some buddies and I tried to go to a warehouse party in the city. We failed. The music was good and the people were good and the outfits were good, but there was no sky. We looked up and all we could see was a roof. Eventually we all piled outside so the smokers could smoke. 'It's weird being in a building,' said Kylz. 'I just feel so hemmed in.'

We did eventually have a good night, but partying needs night sounds, stars, cloud and thick, thumping bass.

Because it just does.

Mother

After dinner, we go out for the evening. Evenings are when things happen, says Chris. Days are fine, but it's evening when the real action starts. It's getting darker, and everyone is walking towards the huge open area. A smell of marijuana hangs over everything. It's a nice smell (fortunately), much more attractive than ordinary cigarettes. I see (worse, smell) only one person smoking an ordinary cigarette in all my five days at HipHaven. There's not much alcohol, either. Men were bringing in cartons of beer, but they seem to drink it at their camps, not in public. It's getting colder as the sun sets, and not so many people are naked. Instead they're wearing every garment imaginable, from gauzy skirts and feathered headbands to dark blue officers' greatcoats with shiny brass buttons.

Once a man wore a suit, for effect, says Chris. Everyone ignored him.

First to the chai tent, a HipHaven institution, beautifully oriental with seductive lights, middle-eastern drapes, red and gold cushions, and Persian-looking carpets. Lovely hot chai, with chat going on all around us. 'I passed in Psychology, but I only got a terminating pass in Philosophy.' 'We stopped the night at Cooma to see my aunty, not far out of the way and boy, does she cook a good roast.' 'I get sick of swearing. It's meaningless, so unimaginative.' Well, I'm agreeing with everything so far. It's surprising — but everything's surprising.

Chris sees lots of friends. 'Hi, Mum!' they all say warmly. 'Hey, Chris's mum's here!' Then to the fire-twirling, a magnificent display of whirling bodies, clothes, balls of flame. They haven't had fire-twirling for years, Chris tells me. Fire-twirling is a hotbed of ferocious passion. People poach in each other's territory, sleep with each other's partners, quarrel, fight, argue, shout ... But something happened, they've decided to have another go, promised to be good, and here they are in front of us, making magic. A beautiful, serene raven-haired woman in a floating indigo skirt twirls the fiery batons effortlessly, creating fabulous mystic patterns against the starlit sky. Surely such a goddess could never argue? Men with flamboyant six-packs, shiny with sweat, carelessly toss around bars of fire. In the background people are drumming, thud-thud-thud tap-tap-tap, faster and faster, louder and louder. Fire, drumming, darkness, flames, and over everything the heady smell of marijuana.

It's all very stunning, but after an hour or so there's a certain sameness, I admit to myself. The throbbing drums, the beautiful twirls of fire, the happy murmur of people in the warm evening — they continue, but they don't develop. And I'm not so good at standing any more. I wonder if Chris wants a bit of time out? I tell her I'm going back to the campsite, and find my way with a fair bit of difficulty, along the paths with potholes which don't show up very clearly in torchlight. The long drop is fine, but I'm extremely careful not to drop the torch in it. Where's the turn-off? Ah, here, the tent with the Chinese lantern hanging from it — thanks, kind campers. Our tent at last. Home. I don't think I'll come back in the dark again.

I unearth the whiskey Laura's partner provided, pour a bit into a cup and sit in my cosy chair, under the canopy of stars, listening to the distant (thank God, goddess or what have you) drumming. I ponder. I'm completely out of my comfort zone. I know my comfort zone very well. It's lovely. It's in Hobart, where I was born and have lived most of my life. There I'm familiar with everything I do, everywhere I go, and a good many of the people I meet. I sang in a choir with that woman, played hockey against this one, was a fellow parent at primary school with another. That man I often see in the grocery, this one I interviewed for such-and-such a book. Good heavens, that's Tom — I went out with him in first year uni. He's still got that long bony nose, which got in the way. Someone coped better than I did, and he's taking his grandchildren to the playground. It's a very comfortable and pleasant world. One, I hardly need add, in which everyone is decently clothed at all times. I write my books, do research in the archives, have lunch with friends, go to concerts and plays, walk in the bush with my husband James, am annoyed by politicians, by nuisance phone calls — but even these pests are familiar.

Here nothing is familiar, except Chris. I'm not sure what to do next, what the routine is, what I should say or do. Not that anyone notices, of course, as I'm the invisible older woman. I never mind this, and I certainly don't now. It makes life so much easier, not being noticed. But the whole thing still makes me feel uncomfortable. It's all just too different. I don't know anyone. But wait a bit, I do. I know the gorgeous Adelaidies. I know about a dozen of

Chris's friends. I can't remember their names, but I know their warm, welcoming faces. I can just muddle along. As long as I'm like everyone else, friendly, open, unjudging, I'll be fine.

Should I give in and go back to the urban comforts of Carlton? It's tempting, for a second. But no, I can't. I can't go without being driven by Chris, and she adores HipHaven. I can't possibly make her leave early, when she's taken so much trouble to get things I like and takes so much pride in me being here. No, I'm staying. For 118 hours, I work out. I've been here for 12. Only 106 to go.

Darling Chris thinks I'm a hippie, but I've only ever been a fringe one, really. I did tell the kids great stories. After uni I went to Europe for two years like people did, and I came home on the Hippie Trail through Asia with an English friend, Mary. Three months hitch-hiking, going on local buses, eating amazing food if it was cheap, crossing dodgy borders, sleeping in all sorts of unusual places, like under a table. There were lots of hippies around, true, but the only hippie-like thing Mary and I did was to have some hash, and that was accidental. In Nepal a man gave us a chocolate brownie each, and we ate them walking in the forest. After a while we started to feel peculiar, like coming out of a faint, but it went on and on and on. We lay down under the trees and waited for it to go. If this was drugs, we said to each other, we couldn't imagine why people took them. It was horrible. But I was on the hippie trail so I was adventurous, and then I took the children to things that were a bit left of centre like protests, and went nude swimming with Chris, so I can see why she thinks I'm unconventional and hippie-like. What she doesn't realise is that people tend to get less adventurous as they get older, and I'm not sure how I'm going to cope with all this.

But I can escape. Not with whiskey, as I didn't like to take too much, but with Agatha. I dig around and find the books I bought this morning — only this morning, but it seems like a decade ago. *Death in the Clouds*: wonderful. I've read every Agatha Christie several times, and this is one of my favourites. Death by a little-known South American poison, painted on a dart, blown with unerring accuracy across a plane. Lots of clever red herrings, in the fascinating setting of a flight from London to Paris in 1936, with barley sugar to suck and cotton wool for your ears, and only about a dozen passengers. A highly unlikely plot — you can't expect our Agatha to be likely; as far as I can see, likely murders are boring and easily solved — so it's time to suspend disbelief and any sense of reality. One way and another, I'll be pretty experienced at this by the time I leave HipHaven.

Chris brought a big old torch, one you wind up. It gives marvellous light for ten minutes and then you have to wind it up again. But who cares: I settle down under the stars to escape into another world with Agatha. Partying noises — shouting, singing, drumming — reverberate in the background, but I'm oblivious. The plane's taking off ...

Daughter

I have lain awake many nights worrying about taking Mum to HipHaven. Her hips are a postmodern construction of titanium and artificial bone, and she must not fall. If she does, we are seventy-six kilometres from the nearest hospital. She is Tasmanian and doesn't like heat, and although the Easter festival is usually calm and quite cool, the temperature may spike into the thirties. There is a nasty blue-green algal bloom. The river, usually the colour of weak milky coffee, is now a virulent pea-soup green, and swimming brings a risk of itchiness and gastro.

Most HipHaveners are lovely, but there are a number of crashingly boring old men with scraggly grey ponytails, and Mum would not cope with them at all. I have several I am trying to avoid: a guy called BrightMoon who considers himself a shamanic healer and latches onto young women, a guy called Gerhart who considers himself a bringer of European wisdom to the masses and latches onto young women, and a guy called Henry who is a fountain of detailed, yet questionable wisdom on everything bar his own inappropriate sexual behaviour, and latches onto young women.

The absolute maximum age of the women these guys attach themselves to is thirty-two, and fortunately Mum and I are well past that now. Beyond that you drop off their radar screens and become invisible. When I was in range, I wasn't particularly bothered by them because I had worked in factories and smelters from the age of eighteen and one of my best-developed skills that I don't put on my resume is the ability to get rid of creepy old sleazebags (of whom there have been many), briskly and effectively although not necessarily gently. If you can manage to break their atmosphere of cosy mateship, they move on quite quickly and find a softer target. But you have to be horrible. They don't respond to polite requests to leave. They don't stop talking just because you're going somewhere else.

Mum is also well out of range, but they do come up and start talking and refuse to stop. Although Mum has chaired a number of committees and has the capacity to be very firm, these old guys have a way of ruining your day. And I don't want them to ruin Mum's, particularly at the start, before she has found her feet.

Balanced against our collective misanthropy when it comes to old guys with inappropriate senses of entitlement is a concern that I have too many friends. This isn't because of being particularly popular or special, it's through repetition: even if you only make friends with two new people per festival, after sixteen festivals you will have thirty-two friends and you will bump into them in the loo queue and at the communal kitchen and all over the place. And they're not just friends; they're festival buddies.

I get heat stress. That means I roll along just fine in the heat until at some point my insides turn into a glowing coal that can't cool down. I find the only real cure is sleep — pressing my body's 'reset' button. And a couple of litres of water and some protein don't hurt, either. There is also a spookily effective mix of cordial, salt and half an aspirin that tends to prevent it from happening. Anyway, at one of the hot festivals I went and did some outdoor jobs like a lunatic, sat on the front gate for a couple of hours. Then when I got dropped back in camp, I realised I couldn't reach my tent without the heat stress reaching its next stage, which is passing out and spewing. So I sort of started staggering along until I saw Larry's van. Larry wasn't there, so I climbed inside and fell asleep on his bed. A while later, I awoke as he returned. 'I got heat stress,' I said. 'Your van rescued me.'

Larry gave me water and hydration salts until I was OK to go back to my own camp. That's a festival buddy. Sometimes we scab food off one another and steal each other's mugs and listen to one another fight with friends and/or partners in public. We also help and rescue one another. We are joined together in snacks and rolling papers and lent loo rolls. We have talked each other through the lean years when mental health was thin on the ground. We've swum naked together and had long talks in the chai tent about everything. The buddies are therefore not a random collection but a singing network of support.

It can be very tiring being the friend, or in this case the mum, of a person like that. 'Oh hey Ants, hey Ants, this is my mum, she came up from Tassie. Mum, Ants and I have known each other for years hahaha, remember that time when we rafted down the river singing I am the Walrus and it was forty-six degrees.' To avoid this, I'll need to keep away from the network a bit. I'm hoping to spend time with Mum in less social places, like our camp, and make friends together with people I don't already know.

Mum is a hippie and she hides beneath a veneer of respectability. She likes clothes in rich colours and women's history and she loves people and their quirks. She also has a strong network of good friends and I can't count the number of times I've seen something at HipHaven and thought, 'Mum would absolutely love this.' So I am looking forward to the time I see her eyes light up at some new curiosity, when she says, 'look, darling, what IS that man wearing?'

FRIDAY

Morning

Mother

'If anyone in this camp's going to murdered, it's the child with the bicycle bell', I mutter to Chris the next morning.

It's been a tough night. The off-the-ground bed Chris promised me is a camp stretcher. Those camp stretchers. They might be above the ground, but they're hard. Even with a camping mattress on top. Hard on the fake hips. The middle-of-the-night loo trek was hideous. You don't want to know more. And I wake to the frightful din of a child's bicycle bell. Before I went to bed I put in earplugs which drowned out the partying noise, but they've fallen out, and this child is riding along the path behind my tent and back again, ringing her bell regularly and enthusiastically. Luckily, the baby in the other tent has been silent.

Anyway, nature calls, so I get dressed. Chris said 'Bring clothes that are out there', so I tried. Friends chipped in — Fran added a golden scarf, Diane a wonderful blue peasant blouse. I put on the red hippie floral happy pants Chris gave me ages ago, an orange T-shirt and Fran's scarf.

Fortunately, as I leave the tent Onyx, the bell-ringer, is at the other end of the path and I manage to avoid glowering. I walk five minutes to the long drops, and the people in the queue are friendly, and the sun streams down between the trees, the birds carol away, and it's all very serene. By the time I get back I'm happy. Onyx has been transformed into an angel in a rainbow dress, fair hair shining in the sunlight, sitting at a table quietly colouring in.

Daughter

Latrines. They are legal in New South Wales above the hundred-year flood mark. Not in Victoria, which is partly why we all have to drive such a stinking long way to get here. Sometimes, like this time, patronage is low and the weather is mild and all is relatively well. Some years, though, there's a stick covered in unmentionable goo resting a discreet way from the arts beach long drops. Inside a long drop, excrement and loo paper fall in a conical shape, and the tip of the cone meets the base of the can before ever the sides of the hole are full. So at a private and early hour, volunteers of a certain toughness circle in and distribute the piles more evenly to make room for another day's deposit. And then Vic and his backhoe sometimes just dig more latrines, a hot and difficult job, but one that keeps the festival rolling and provides a means to our ends.

There is no shitty stick this year, as the festival is quiet and small and I am grateful for the cleanliness and absence of chaos and for Vic and his helpers and their contributions in the past, as I wash my hands, walk back to camp and put on the billy.

Mother

Chris has the kettle boiling for tea. I know she prefers herbal or green, but she's making black for me, the dear girl. We discuss last night — chai and coffee, the fire twirling in the darkness, the chanting, the enthusiasm.

She kept on for hours, being young. I tell her it was a funny old night here. The earplugs are pretty good but they don't keep out everything. No, says Chris, they let in nearby voices in case someone is warning you of fire. Well, one nearby voice last night was singing, of all things, 'O come all ye faithful'. 'Shut the fuck up with that damned Christmas carol!' shouted someone. At Hiphaven! Not very tolerant. Tut tut.

Beyond Chris, a neighbouring camper is playing the flute. Jethro Tull: I know because it says so on his music book (I like classical myself, one thing I'll never hear at this festival). We applaud, and he introduces himself. He's in his fifties, Ron from Brisbane, and he sleeps in a fascinating little coffin-like tent which he likes because you can lie in the open and look at the stars. Unlike us, he's a minimalist camper with a small esky and a tiny bag and little else. He has three clothing options: shirt and shorts, a poncho or nothing. 'What do you do in Brisbane?' I ask. He works in the Tax Office. Here is a man naked under a poncho, playing the flute, telling me he's a serious and doubtless utterly respectable public servant in his other life. He plays 'Jerusalem' and I sing along, and we both get quite carried away.

Our other neighbour emerges from his tent. We apologise for waking him up but he says, politely, that he was awake already. He's American, in his twenties, Andy from California, charming and courteous in that well-bred American way (his father turns out to be an international lawyer). He's backpacking around Australia, going to festivals. It's his first HipHaven, but Ron's a regular. He doesn't tell his children, saying he's going to visit friends. 'Well, you're my friends', he says. 'It's true.' We share some grapes with him and Andy, who seems to have no food at all.

I don't want to irritate Chris by being with her all the time and the nearby baby has started crying, so I go off to the Craft Cafe. This is a large tarpaulin over an area full of chairs, balls of wool, baskets of material and so on. I noticed it yesterday and thought it looked promising. Chris said there would be workshops, and I'd as soon do craft as anything, while the 'café' bit sounds good too (Chris doesn't drink coffee). There's a workshop on garland making. I imagine knitting a Hawaiian lei, but the garland's for a commitment ceremony this afternoon (wedding, in mundane English). We're crocheting flowers to attach to a long green rope, as a decoration. There's Sue, Jenny, Chantelle and Vivienne. Others come and go but we're the stayers, crocheting away for several hours, talking and drinking coffee. Sue is lively, with dark curly hair, and I like her at once. Chantelle is English and plump, which is unusual at HipHaven where hardly anyone's overweight. Well, you wouldn't come to a clothing-optional festival, would you? Chantelle looks striking: jet-black dyed hair, a dark red velvet skirt and a startling purple and gold scarf with sequins. All the women at the craft café are wearing clothes, mostly beautiful floaty skirts and dresses, scarves and wraps, in lovely colours. Gentle Vivienne, in shades of blue, could be the high priestess of a cult of some benign goddess who brings tranquillity to all around.

These women know their craft. We discuss crochet needles and Jenny brings out her prized one, very pretty in rainbow colours. We all admire it. I'd thought of many possible things I'd be doing at HipHaven, but admiring crochet needles wasn't one of them — though that's fine. At least it's something I can do, with zest if necessary. People finish flowers, and Chantelle starts sewing them on to the rope. We chat about craft, and other workshops, and someone brings more coffee. The other women are old hands at HipHaven, been coming for years. I like them. They're in their forties and fifties, and their talk is interesting, vibrant. No one is telling me about her children, let alone grandchildren, a huge bonus. I ask what they do back home. Physio, drama teacher, Health Department, accountant, they tell me.

I've been knitting since childhood but I've never learnt to crochet. Sue teaches me the basic moves and I manage to make a long purple strand, but she's too busy to continue the lessons. I move to a plastic flower-weaving gadget, the sort of thing you'd give a struggling six-year-old for occupational therapy: but it's something I can do, and it's satisfying in its way.

'I'm a bit disappointed in your names', I say. They look surprised. 'Sue, Jenny, Chantelle — where are the hippie names, the' — I just stop myself saying 'weird' — 'the unusual ones?'

They laugh and dredge their memories, but they can't think of many. Sue knows someone called O-Shaan (say it aloud). There's Osiris and Zeus. What would you call Zeus as a nickname? I tell them about Onyx and Nimrod. These women's children are called names like Sam and Isabel — and they're not at HipHaven. Kids are brought when they're little, but once they're about eleven, they get embarrassed and that's it. They stay at home with Granny, who gives them chops for dinner and never goes round nude.

Jenny, who's lovely and kind, tells me about another nude commitment ceremony last year. The groom's family, Israelis, were stunned by it, couldn't cope with the nudity, especially the 86-year-old grandmother. But next day, Jenny saw her in the painting tent, nude from the waist up, being painted by children, tears rolling down her face. 'This has changed my life forever', she told Jenny. I barely control a snort. (Laura doesn't even try. 'Time running out, not much choice, if she's going to transform her life she had to pick *something* pretty quickly.') Chantelle tells us she gave up her work in the real world, teaching, to travel the globe going to festivals. 'This is the real life', she says whimsically. For God's sake, I want to say, who do you think pays for you to do this — taxpayers providing you with the dole! At least they're English taxpayers.

People wander by and chat. There's one old man I take a dislike to. He's wearing a T-shirt with a large stylised eye and the wording: 'Highly evolved people have their own conscience as pure law'. What the hell does that mean? I have no idea, except that obviously he thinks he's highly evolved. Well, I can tell he's not, because he's got long grey hair in a pony tail, straggly but immaculately combed. I'm wary of old men with long grey hair. I've found from experience that they're mostly nutters. He comes and leers over Sue as she's crocheting, says something I can't hear, and Sue sends him off pretty quick smart. 'Henry', she shrugs to us. 'Old sleaze-bag. I hate these dreadful old lechers. I wish they could keep them out of HipHaven. There aren't many, but they spoil it for the rest of us.'

This starts a discussion on individual freedom, and also on young women's freedom not to be sleazed on. There's, not exactly an argument, but certainly animated discussion, between ardent feminists led by Sue and ardent civil libertarians led by Chantelle. What happens when people's rights and civil liberties coincide? Sue's telling us how appallingly her ex-husband behaves, challenging the civil libertarians. She's a good arguer and even Chantelle is floundering.

Hannah joins us, a breezy, cheerful woman. To a comment I can't hear she replies, 'Oh, that community crap! I'm sick of it!' I gasp. At HipHaven! She catches my eye and grins. 'I've been in collectives. They're usually so badly run. A committee of well-meaning people can't manage things. What you need is a benevolent dictator.' She chuckles. So strong is her personality that everyone agrees. Yes, a benevolent dictator does organise things well, get things done, we murmur.

Needing a little break from all this and a leg-stretch, I take my coffee mug to wash it. Chantelle and Vivienne are standing by the sink. 'My opinion should have been asked', Chantelle says curtly, her sequins flashing. 'I don't want a communal washing-up tub.' Vivienne looks crushed. We return to the crochet and I sit beside her. 'I thought that was quite unnecessary', I say comfortingly. She turns to me gratefully. 'Oh, thank you! I thought it was just me.' 'There are ways to say things, and no need to be grumpy', I continue. I can see a role here: the soother. At last, a niche in HipHaven! I can be the older experienced woman offering comfort, no problem. Still, obviously it's not all sweetness and light here.

I have to be watchful myself. Having cleverly mastered the occupational therapy gadget, I put down a completed flower for the garland, saying lightly, 'Here we go, there's more than one way to ski—' then stop short, appalled at the terrible clanger I've almost dropped. I force out a cough to end my sentence, overdo it, choke, splutter, and there's a few minutes of kind people thumping my back and offering glasses of water. It all calms down.

'What were you saying, Sally?' asks Jenny politely, blast her. But during the coughing I'd been thinking desperately: what else begins with ski—? 'Just an old saying', I say, as lightly as I can. 'There's more than one way to skim cream.'

'That's a funny one', comments practical Hannah. 'I'd think there was only one way.'

Shit! She's right. The pitfalls you dig for yourself! My mind flails around desperately again. Found it! My one advantage over these women is a longer memory. Not necessarily better, in fact surely not better, but it stretches back further. 'I remember skimming cream', I say, adding a nice little wistful tone to my voice to show I'm not in the least worried about dropping clangers — well, at least it will change the ambience, and stop anyone saying she's never before heard my historic adage which is all of ten seconds old. 'You're all probably too young, but when I was about five an old man called Perce used to deliver milk to housewives every morning. Mum and I would walk up the drive with the billy and he'd fill it with a dipper from his big — I can't remember, vat, kerosene tin, container of fresh milk, anyway. I suppose he'd just milked his cows. We'd walk very carefully down the drive with it, one of those rituals of childhood, not spilling a drop, and Mum would put it in the fridge. After a few hours the cream settled on the top and as a treat I was sometimes allowed to skim it.'

'How to get kids to do things!' laughs someone.

'It really was a treat', I say. 'It's very satisfying. As you pushed your tablespoon *very* gently along the *very* top of the milk — Mum's instructions — the cream wrinkled. You'd keep pushing until you had a wonderful dollop of thick cream to lift out and put on the apple pie on Sunday. Then you got another dollop, but you didn't take all the cream or the milk didn't taste nice. Or so we thought then.'

'It can't have been too hard, if your mother let a five-year-old do it', comments Chantelle.

'No', I say, 'and anyway, it's one of those jobs you can fix if a child mucks it up. Cream floats so you can always find any stray lumps, and a bit of milk just makes the cream for the apple pie slightly less solid. So delicious, that thick solid cream! In the days when you were allowed to eat it.'

'So old Perce didn't keep the best of the cream himself?' asks Sue.

'Old Perce's life-long customers would have known the second he started any racket, and raised hell.' I laugh, dizzy with relief. Safe! Sue's helpful comment gives me a perfectly natural escape from skimming damned cream to something far away from it. 'Those were the 1950s, when every penny counted. I remember Mum making one-egg cakes. It's not starvation exactly, but we wouldn't bother today.' The conversation veers off on to other mothers' much more interesting economies than the one I frantically dredged up from the murky depths of memory, and I relax back into the general cosiness. My exhausted brain needs a little rest.

I'm startled into full alert as somehow or other this conversation leads to Vivenne telling me she paints with her menstrual blood. I'm so taken aback I can scarcely get a word out, but utterly fascinated. I'm dying to ask questions. Curiosity wins. 'How do you collect it?' I ask. In a special little cup, she says. I'm agog. 'Doesn't it start coagulating?' Yes, it does, so you have to be fast. 'You couldn't really do a big painting, could you?' No, but there's beauty in miniature. It doesn't seem polite to continue, but I want to keep on — you wouldn't get much at once, do you keep on getting more through your period and add to the painting? How do you vary the shade — dried blood isn't a very exciting colour. No, no, Sally, wrong, you're being judgmental, all colours have their own beauty. Just as well I didn't actually say that. Unfortunately Vivienne hasn't any of the paintings with her.

I make four flowers, and sew the purple strand into a type of flower, if you look at it from a distance with your eyes blurred — but good thoughts go with it and that has to be the main thing, doesn't it? Then I go back to the campsite for lunch. No, Chris tells me, it's not all sweetness at HipHaven. People get cross, just like home. There's an area without drink or drugs or loud noise, and they're super bossy. Once in the cooking area Chris had bacon, and got really told off by a vegetarian. She doesn't go there any more, even though she's not into drink or drugs.

Dimly through the earplugs last night I thought I heard an ambulance siren, and I ask Chris about it. Yes, it was an ambulance. Three people were taken to hospital because a dealer sold them bad acid. The camp organisers gave him five minutes to pack, then dumped him on the highway halfway to the nearest town. It happens at night, Chris says, after people like me go to bed.

Then, keeping my voice down, I tell Chris about how the craft cafe nearly heard that there's more than one way to skin a cat. 'At HipHaven, a terrible thing to say! Hurtful to vegetarians let alone vegans, animal lovers, peace followers, anti-violence people, the lot.'

Chris is amused. 'But you know', she adds, 'Hannah was wrong. There are more ways that one to skim cream. You can use a milk separator.'

Daughter

One year, they ran a drug bust on both roads leading into the festival. Luckily my friend Lizzie and I were the first of our buddies to get done, and we were clean and sober and cheerful, hadn't a skerrick of a drug in the car which, helpfully, was a sky blue mini 4wd that looked like it had just driven out of a bayside suburb. The cops didn't take us seriously and strolled the dogs round our car at a small distance. The dogs looked at the cops, like, 'Why are you wasting my time?' and they let us through.

We, of course, popped round the corner, pulled over and warned everyone via facebook while our phones were still in range. The buddies employed a number of devious methods to arrive safely — one drove through the night and came through the blockade right at shift change, having estimated when that would be. He was fine. Others employed the sneaky tactic of leaving their drugs at home.

The festival was then full of dispirited people — one had copped a big fine for taking a Victorian-registered trailer into New South Wales (who knew that was against the law?) and others had had all their stuff chucked out of their cars. There was a sense of violation. People had been fined and were facing criminal records. Also, the cops had arrested everyone's good mate Negri, who had a stack of drugs in his van. Negri was mourned by all and the cops later put him away for two years. 'Oh, poor Negri,' said everyone. 'It's a terrible thing. He's so young.' Pause. 'Mind you, he was driving around with a bloody shitload of drugs, though.'

Halfway through the festival, I went and spoke to the organisers, who were in their secret camp (it's away from the other campers, screened off by shadecloth) looking surprisingly relaxed. They were sitting on lawn furniture in a circle with beers, and for once they had their feet up. 'Pretty terrible about this drug bust, eh?' I said.

'Hah!' they chorused. 'First aid calls are down by half! Fights are down by even more! This is the best festival ever! We want them to run a drug bust every time!' And they chuckled into their beers. I was a bit taken aback by their heartlessness in the face of the suffering of the patrons, but I could see that when you're the sucker that has to deal with all the fights and first aid calls, not having to deal with them would be pretty damn great.

New Year's Eve that year was a shemozzle. There were people roving around with desperate, keen expressions, unable to source ecstasy or mushies, or even dope. People were asking me where they could find drugs, which meant they were completely stumped. Actually, things became so rampant, even I knew where the drugs were, because a girl had a little bag of mushies she was selling, and I'd overheard a conversation with her friend, when they realised they had more than they needed for the night. I hope she turned a decent profit. However, a lot of people were left alone with their emotions for that party.

I was going through a bout of depression and couldn't find a way to lose the thousand-yard stare, so I apprenticed myself to a guy called Norton and learned to make spuds the famous Norton way. For an incredibly grumpy man, he was surprisingly soothing to work with, given that I felt like rubbish. There are no holds barred, conversationally, he's honest at a level most people aren't. I was free to stand around pricking potatoes and putting them on trays or grinding spices. No one needed me to be fun or cheerful or emotionally present. I'd recommend it.

Lunch

Mother
Back at the campsite, Chris and I have a salad for lunch, with all the delicious bits and pieces Chris brought.

She's a very good camper. It comes from living in the Western Australian outback for years, but also from her strong streak of common sense and a feeling for intuitive knowledge. My grandmother was like that, very capable. She could have run an empire, but instead she ran a farm and family and husband who'd been gassed in the First World War so his lungs were shot, and got them through the Depression. 'It's enough to make a monkey bite its mother', was her favourite saying, and her monkey must have worn out its teeth through those tough years. By the time I knew her, experience had given her a fund of stories about how she gave advice that invariably turned out right. She always knew how to do things, and she was full of advice. 'Never boil a stew. Just let it simmer.' How true, I've often thought, as I forget to turn a stew down and there it is, boiling away like mad, going all stringy. 'When you're bottling fruit, always pick it ripe', she used to say. 'Some people pick it green because it's neater, but it's taste you want, not neatness.' Not so useful any more — though as a general principle, taste not neatness is pretty good. I expect she also had sound advice about making calves' foot jelly and home-made vegemite. Anyway, Chris is capable in just the same way.

She's worked out how to keep fruit and vegetables fresh. You get a large plastic container, and put about an inch of water in the bottom. Them you stand things like lettuce and celery upright in it, and put other things in as well. You cover it with a wet sarong or tea towel, and put it in the shade. Evaporation means the fruit and veg stays crisp and fresh. It doesn't work inside a house, Chris says, but it works perfectly here. You do have to keep wetting the sarong.

Andy has wandered off but Ron is there, sitting on his chair. We chat. He seems a bit lonely; if you're a reserved person I imagine HipHaven could be lonely, among all these people being warm and loving to each other, not daring to butt in. I tell him about my craft morning, and he says he's looking for a group to play his flute with. We urge him to play, offering biscuits, and he has another go. There's a kookaburra singing at the same time. It's all very — what's the word — almost medieval. Nothing modern, just Ron and the kookaburra making music and Chris and me appreciating it. Pre-lapsarian comes to mind, but I'm not sure what it means. It has a nice sound, though. Later on I look it up — innocent and unspoilt, that's it exactly.

In the afternoon I decide to avoid the nude commitment ceremony. So does the bride's family: her father is a minister, and they're holding a church wedding next weekend. This is all so weird, with such a dysfunction between Here and Outside. It's like being in some exclusive religion, the same suspension of scepticism needed. But I hope the bride likes her garland.

Instead, Chris and I decide to go to the market.

Daughter

'Aah! You spilled sauce on my jumper!'

'Whoops, sorry about that,' says Andy, our neighbour. We're nearing the market and Andy is with a bunch of young men. His friend is mopping at Andy's stomach with a serviette in a frenzied sort of way.

'First you steal it and then you ruin it!'

'I borrowed it out of your car. I couldn't see mine. Or did I not bring one? I don't know. Anyway, I'll clean it and bring it back to you.'

'I can't believe you call yourself my friend.'

'I do feel awful. Oh, hey.' He sees me and strolls over. 'Hey neighbour! How's it going?'

'Great!'

'Apart from you've got sauce on your friend's jumper.'

'He'll get over it.'

'He doesn't look happy.'

'Don't start him again.'

'What are you up to? Pulling chicks?'

'Oh no. We're just hanging.'

'Coz there's loads of them down at the beach,' I say, helpfully. 'Naked.'

'Oh, I don't do that. I don't like the vibe.'

'Oh, OK.' I can never understand it when attractive people aren't sleazebags. Seems weird to me. Like a waste or something. 'Are you sure, because there's totally a steam tent...'

'Hah! Nah.' He looks quietly down. Swallows his cheeks.

'OK, have it your way. So where are you going?'

'I'm helping these guys set up their camps, and then we're going to a sound healing workshop.'

'Oh, I love those. Have a good time!'

'Yeah, you too.'

'See ya back at the ranch!'

'Will do.'

It seems peculiar that Mother Nature could spit out trashbags like my friend Gordon and guys like Andy on the same planet.

I catch up with Mum and follow her into the market, looking for stuff to buy. At work, I've seen a photo of a woman in a tomb. She had died 2000 years ago and been buried wearing her gold bracelets. Now she was dust and bones, and on those dusty armbones her bangles shone as bright and perfect as if the burial had happened the day before. She had decayed, and they had not. I realised that all my metal-and-stone jewellery would outlive me. So today I'm on the lookout for something made of wood. Something that will decay with me. Something that won't laugh at my puny lifespan.

Mother

I want to buy a souvenir of HipHaven to show my friends, who are all keen to know how I'm getting on. We wander through the camp, past the long drops, the permaculture people, the hug pit which is always empty, the First Aid place, and arrive at the row of tents. The first one is jewellery, intriguing stuff ranging from feathered headbands (Paris courtesan rather than Native American, so that's all right) to necklaces and rings. Rings! I love rings. There's a wonderful one of lapis lazuli and white shell. 'How much?' I ask the woman on the stall, an amazing sight in a long orange garment with a silver scarf, a feathered headdress and heavy make up. This is unusual for HipHaven. Most women, including me, don't even wear a touch of lippy.

'Don't know, love, I'm just minding it for Shakra.' So Chris and I try things on and chat to the stall minder, Nicky. She's forthright. 'Yeah, looks good.' 'Nah, terrible. Take it off.' Finally Shakra turns up, an enchantingly pretty and ethereal young woman, just the sort to be working with lapis lazuli and shell. She too looks blank when asked a price. 'How much do you want to pay?' Eventually, after a bit of polite to- and fro-ing, we settle on a figure. This is HipHaven, isn't it, non-commercial, friendly, consensual. The ring's a bit big and set crookedly, but who cares.

Once again, along comes that frightful old man, Henry. Well, I call him old. He's probably much the same age as I am, but there's something about sleaziness that looks old. Chris and I look at each other. 'He's like the bad spirit of HipHaven', I mutter back. 'Always turning up when he's not wanted.' This time his T-shirt has a large picture of a snarling wolf, with the words, 'Fear makes the wolf bigger than he is'. I'm sure Henry loves going round being a wolf. Though won't the message encourage people to stand up to him? He probably can't think that far. He comes into the stall and leers over Shakra, saying something I can't hear. Of course I can't. It isn't meant for me. Shakra looks helpless. Nicky's fiddling away behind the stall, but she senses something's up and comes charging out, an orange knight in shining armour to the rescue. 'Bugger off', she says to Henry. 'Take your prick to someone who wants it. As if.' He looks aghast, and vanishes. 'Don't put up with it, love,' Nicky tells Shakra. 'Men like that, they take advantage of you. Out for what they can get. Bastards, the lot of them.'

Chris and I potter round the stalls. Camel-hide shoes, made by a charming Afghan man. The camel hide is beautifully soft. Home-made cosmetics. All sorts of wafty clothes in beautiful natural dyes. They probably aren't really, but they look like it. I'm tempted to buy a man-kilt for my husband James, just to see his face when he opens the parcel, but common sense prevails: what a waste of money. Chris tries things on while I watch. At home I'd be working, taking a brief time off for tea, then straight back to the computer, hard at it. Here time doesn't matter. I haven't been anywhere with that attitude for decades.

A friend of Chris's comes up. Chris introduces me. 'How do you do?' he says. I can hardly believe my ears. 'How do you do'! My grandmother used to insist we say that because it was polite, but I haven't heard it for ages. And at HipHaven! This is the weirdest place of contrasts and mismatches anywhere in the entire world. Just as I thought I was getting the hang of it, too.

Chris decides to buy a scarf for a friend, but there's no stall keeper. We poke around, look through gaps in the tent, give a few tentative calls. Nothing. There's a man on a banana lounge outside the tent, smoking a joint. 'She's away. I'm minding the stall', he says lazily. But like Nicky, he has no idea of what to charge. We decided $20 is fair, and leave it with him. I hope he remembers it.

By now I'm flagging. Time to go home. We go back to the car to get some more of our stuff, especially my inflatable airbed. Friends had warned me against camp stretchers and advised this as insurance. Thank goodness. It's a bit of a pest carrying it all back to the campsite, but no pain no gain, all that sort of thing, and we fix it all up eventually. And it's wonderful, doing all these things with Chris. We work together well, always have.

Daughter

I didn't see quite the wood and leather thing I had in mind, which pretty much never happens when you go shopping with an idea in your head of what you want to buy. Mum turns to me. 'I need to go home,' she says. So we go, arm in arm. It's a wonderful feeling, having Mum here. You might think it's a departure to take someone who is in her sixties with rebuilt hips to the bush to party with a bunch of younger people, but in fact this is what we have always done. Not this specific thing, but going on adventures together. One of my earliest memories is of her saying, 'swim to Mummy!' and me swimming a tiny distance into the v of her waiting arms. We learned to swim quite young and then went boogie-boarding at increasingly challenging locations until at thirteen I was watching her catch enormous dumping waves on an inflatable surf mat. We even had our own language for surfing: waves were 'a bit tijjy,' (Mum's phrasing) if they were too small, or 'too round' and then 'walls' when they were too big. If we weren't getting any waves, we'd pray to Poseidon. We had a conversational relationship with Poseidon — Mum would look beyond the breakers and say, 'Come on Possie, send us a wave!' I'm not sure that Poseidon was used to being nicknamed, he probably hadn't had many Australian devotees before, but he sent us plenty of great waves so it can't have hurt.

When people talk about what got them through puberty, for me it was long walks with Mum, where we started talking when we got into the car, talked two hours to the carpark, all the way up the mountain, sat on the mountaintop talking through lunch and then talked our way back down. Puberty is difficult and talking is one way through it. I told her about how much marijuana there was around, what kids were doing and how I felt about it. I may have disclosed some of my teenage crushes. Probably. Mum told me about her books and who she had interviewed. Some people think that women working is a bad thing, but Mum has inspired me. Through her work, she gave me a reference point for workplace contentment. After finishing university, I would look at the job I was in and think, 'Am I happy?'

As a kid, now and again I'd come home and Mum would be full of news about how she'd interviewed a woman who was in her nineties, and still had all her marbles, and as a child the old woman had walked to the market with two buckets of raspberries and it would take several days to get there and now and again she'd stop and stir the mouldy raspberries in with a stick. And I'd think, 'yuck!' and, 'that sounds like a long way to go with two buckets of raspberries,' and, 'I wonder if people noticed the stirred-in mouldy ones?' and, 'kids like me must seem like awful wimps to that old woman'.

When gauging happiness, I would think, 'It didn't happen every day. But now and again, does doing this work fill me with excitement of the sort that Mum had?' and the answer would always be no. So I kept looking and looking for better lines of work until now I'm in a job where I come home sometimes and say to whoever's in the kitchen, 'Guess what I found out today?'

So we walk gingerly back, arm in arm. I hope there isn't a root to trip over. Perhaps there's a god in Poseidon's pantheon I should be praying to, some land-based god of roots and balance. I think secretly, I already did and was reassured that all would be well.

Mother

After a cup of tea, Chris goes off for the afternoon.

I sit back, gazing at the trees, thinking of Chris as a baby. Her birth was cataclysmic for me and James. There you are, more or less in control of your life, knowing what you should be doing and having a go at it — and suddenly, here's this newcomer utterly dependent on you for everything, and you don't know what to do. All the books of advice, antenatal classes, experts, mothers and friends do their best, but really, it's an enormous, irrevocable step into the unknown.

That was my first year teaching, in a pretty tough high school. I liked the kids. They said what they thought, which gave a bit of direction, unlike my Diploma of Education. But I didn't feel I was helping them much, despite trying my hardest. My subjects were French and Social Science. French cut little ice, and in Social Science I had to teach a lot of topics I knew nothing about: The Law and You (zilch), Our Constitution (not much more), Advertising (ditto — Mum and Dad were strictly non-commercial television only) and Sex Education. We didn't have sex education when I was young. Mum gave me a pamphlet which by some weird process led me to understand that sex was a clinical action, necessary but trying, done standing in front of the mantelpiece. At school there was nothing much. We had to extrapolate from dissecting a rabbit in Biology.

The authorities did have one try, the Licked Cakes fiasco. Debate rages among my former classmates about whether the cakes were licked or nibbled, or even bitten, but I'm in the Licked group. When we were in Grade 8, aged about thirteen, runs this oft-told-after-dinner story, the nun in charge of the order (austere Anglican, not jolly Catholic) visited the school, and swept into our classroom. She started on a talk I sensed was about something you didn't mention, which made me feel uncomfortable, though I had no idea what she was talking about. Perhaps it was keeping ourselves pure, something like that? But all very obscure. Then came the memorable sentence, even more obscure. 'Now, girls', she said, 'if you were walking along the street and saw a shop window with a row of iced cakes, would you buy them if they had already been licked?' I was a literal child. Cakes in shops never had been licked, so what she was talking about? It was even less helpful than extrapolating from the rabbit's internal organs.

I had to pick up sex education as I went along, and this was what I was trying to impart to these poor kids when I myself got pregnant accidentally. How I don't know. I was on the pill, but I suppose I forgot it. We had no idea when Chris was due, since it took me a while to work out I was pregnant. We thought it might be January. About a month before the possible birth date, we were having friends to dinner. At six o'clock I had just got the food ready, the table set, and the plates in the oven, when my waters broke. After I realised what had happened, which took a few minutes since I didn't have much idea of anything, I rang the doctor. 'Go to hospital', he said. 'I can't, we've got people coming to dinner.' There was a sigh at the other end of the phone. 'Go to hospital', he repeated, slowly and clearly. So we rang one of the guests with the news to pass around, and drove off. At least James had plenty to eat for the next few days.

Mercifully I can't remember much about the labour, except that it was a forceps birth. Ouch! But it was reasonably short, and Chris was born about midnight, a little pink body placed on mine. 'What time was she born?' asked the doctor. We all looked at the clock: five past twelve. 'Five to twelve', said James firmly. He said later he thought the further away from Christmas a child's birthday was, the better. But it's no good for astrology, Chris, not knowing what minute you were born, let alone which day.

We named the baby Christine, because it was a family name and because we thought it had a good ring. Being three weeks early (they calculated) she had jaundice, her dear little body an odd shade of yellow which made my heart ache. She had to spend a lot of time under lights, and I couldn't see her much. Finally after ten days they let us take her home: James and me with Chris in a basket, James driving with a set, grim expression, me quaking about what to do next with the baby. Halfway home we got a flat tyre. 'I'm not stopping!' said James curtly, so we drove on, thud-thud-thud, for about five minutes until we reached the house.

My next memory is that night, lying in bed rigid, listening to the baby breathe. In — wait, wait, wait, will she keep going — thank heavens, out. After about half an hour James said 'I can't stand it', and carried the basket to the sitting room, closing the door. But we loved her, of course we adored her. I kept thinking, she's too young to remember my mistakes. Which proved right. It wasn't anything too frightful, anyway, except the time I pinned her beautiful baby flesh to the nappy. It was mainly only incompetence, which was useful in preparing her for life in general. Like whatever she's doing out in HipHaven at the moment.

Daughter

I head off to the arts village. Mum's in her chair with a novel. Near the beach I see Dave, Arts beach Dave. Most people think festivals just happen, you rock up one day and there they are, but it's very much not the case. Dave and others like him make the festivals happen. He's a wiry senior citizen and committed nudist who tells it like it is. 'I've put in about fifty days' work,' he says. 'We had a big build this year. We've been expecting a lot of people. The algae knocked us round, we would have had more if that hadn't happened.'

'How many tickets have been sold?' See, this is why you know people. You get in the loop.

'Oh, north of five thousand. We rebuilt the steam tent, and we've siphoned off water for it and the hot tub. It gets filtered through a carbon filter, a zeolite filter and a particle filter. Also, it's getting dosed.'

He means chlorine. I trust him. If anyone can get the algae out of the river water, it's Dave. Also, I expect he's put the inlet from the pump underneath the surface of the water, which is where most of the algae live.

'Thanks for all your effort,' I say. 'I'll come over tomorrow and give you a hand.'

'It's all done now!' he says.

'All the more reason!' I say. But I don't come over later.

I look around and can see everything that has happened — a good clean area for the crew to cook and relax in, a water tank full of triple filtered water, up high so it can gravity feed the arts centre. The steam tent looks new — in years gone by, it was a massive contraption with four wings and a large vestibule to enter by. Now it's smaller and square. I think it's smaller because they don't want to use as much of their water, which is now difficult to come by. Also, they hose out the steam tent and hot tub daily, but now the river water isn't suitable, they will prefer to do less hosing.

Over at the river, people are diving in. You can see once they break the surface that the water underneath is pretty clear. I look on in mild horror. People can't be diving in. What if they get gastro or itchiness? Also, don't some people have severe allergic reactions? Anyway, they are defying my worries and having fun. I want to go too, I want to float on my back in the middle of the stream, watching the trees sway and the sulphur crested cockatoos fly overhead. Stand in the water on a hot day and gossip. This river has seen many conversations. It's probably been here in some form or another since the Great Dividing Range was taller than the Himalayas, three hundred million years ago. This river is why all of inland eastern Australia is flat. It's called an infilled backarc basin, which means there is a chain of mountains by the coast and a bunch of rivers draining the sediment inland and filling the landscape with sand and mud and silt. Underneath us somewhere are the original hills and valleys, but they all got filled in, and the mighty Murray and her sister river, the Edwards, have been part of that. And they flow still, moving milky brown sediment two thousand kilometres to the sea in South Australia. Carrying memories and silt and fertiliser (don't talk to me about fertiliser, bloody algal bloom) and cow shit and litter and the spirit of the land.

This is what I brought Mum to see. When we were growing up, we took small drink bottles on long bushwalks because in Tassie, you can usually drink the creek water, so you can fill up your drink bottle at the streams you pass. Here, you can't, not without getting sick. Apparently you can acclimatise to river water, but I have never thought that would be a good idea. Here, drinkable creek water would be considered a great luxury. It's funny how many luxuries we grew up with without realising it. Clean air, great views. When I go walking in Victoria, I take a lot of water with me. Sometimes if I can see the mountain the creek drains from and it's bush all the way, I've tried drinking the creek water, but I've always got sick. Dull headaches that last a day, a runny tummy. I brought forty litres of rainwater from our tank to HipHaven, so we don't have to drink the processed river water here. It's pretty good this year, but sometimes they need to add so much chlorine, it tastes like they've siphoned it out of a municipal pool and filtered out the band-aids. Mind you, most Victorian tap water tastes like that to me after a couple of years on tank water.

I think we humans have spent hundreds, maybe thousands of years getting essential services to most people, now the challenge will be to deal with the fallout of our civilisation. Businesses to be in over the next hundred years will be filtration (water filters, air filters, ocean cleanup filters) and recycling. We're running low on a lot of metals and we'll need them. The thing is, metal prices will rise as the metals become unavailable, so you can sell them back into the market, but no one will pay you to filter the ocean. If my naturalist friends and I were to trap all the carp in the Murray Darling system so it ran clear again, who would pay?

Dinner

Mother

I chop salad vegetables and open tins, and after dinner Chris heads off for the evening wearing an amazing outfit, capped by a knitted Viking helmet. Truly, a knitted Viking helmet. It has a brown beanie-bit, knitted in a stitch that looks like armour, and then two wonderful knitted white horns, stuffed with something so they stand out firmly. Valhalla, here we come! Whoever thought of knitting a Viking helmet? People are extraordinary, aren't they. What with one thing and another, like thinking about knitting a Viking helmet, I'm quite overcome. It's been a long day.

Daughter

After a tuna salad and some pasta, Mum makes a confession.

'Darling,' she says, 'It's terribly pathetic I know, but I think I'll stay here after dark. I really don't want to fall.'

'OK, Mum,' I say, trying to be reasonable. After all, my number one principle is that Mum must not fall, and that would be much more likely after dark. It is a bit disappointing that she won't be out, because so many lovely things happen at night. And I worry about her eyes because I knew she will be reading in the tent by the inadequate light of my wind-up torch, consuming book after book as the party whirls by her.

The thing is, though, people are in charge of themselves and it's important not to get in their way. I have been lecturing myself about the importance of not being controlling. Especially with Mum, who's the most competent person I know. I arrange some going-out gear, tie-dyed leggings and a shawl and puffy jacket. Arm warmers, boots. After Mum reassures me again that she really is fine, I head out.

My feet lead me to the beach, where a cluster of people stand naked around the fires. They look so wonderful, their bodies gleaming like copper in the firelight. There are no other lights apart from the stars. I strip off my clothes at the logpile and gingerly step into the hot tub. The organisers run the water through a heat exchange that sits over a fire, and the hot inlet pipe is right next to the entrance, making it too warm. I negotiate my way through the bodies to the other end. I am relaxing, looking up at the silhouettes of the trees and letting my shoulders drop, when someone at the other end of the bath asks if anyone has a light. I look over and see a skinny-looking guy with short black hair.

'Huw?' I call.

'Yes?' he says, then sees me walking towards him. 'Chris!' he calls. 'What are you doing in here?'

'This is what I do! You fire twirlers sit in your own little world and never go out, but the rest of us do workshops and the hot tub and the river. What are you doing here?'

'I always come here!'

'Well, why don't I see you?'

'Dunno!'

And we settle in to talk about twirler politics, who is with who, who had which developments in their life since last festival. There isn't a lot to catch up on because we were all at a party at New Year's Eve, and it was stinking hot so we sat round under a tree and caught up fully then. But we love each other, and we've been festival buddies for ten years, and it is wonderful to see him here and sit together in the starlight.

A woman walks past. Her boobs look kind of unrealistic, very round. I try not to stare. 'I love man-made boobies,' says Huw quietly.

'I know what you mean. I'm bisexual, and ...'

'You too?' said Huw.

'What, you're never bi, are you?'

'Yep, for as long as I can remember!' he exclaims. I can't believe I've known him all this time and have never had an inkling. My gaydar must have been malfunctioning.

'I'm kind of fifty-fifty,' I say.

'Yep, right down the middle.'

'I mean, I date nearly all blokes because it's so much easier and the lesbian community can be tricky. But I know myself, I know who I'm interested in. Hey, you're still with Sonja, aren't you?'

'Yes, we've been living together for eight years. There's nothing there any more. I don't think she finds me attractive.'

'Wow, that sucks, dude. You can feel really ugly when your partner isn't interested.'

'Yeah, I do. And I feel really weird coz I like guys too. Like there isn't a place for me. But I don't think I'm wrong. I love humans. Whether they're a guy or a girl just seems totally irrelevant to me.'

'Me too. People ask about being bi, I say to them, do you know whether your next partner will have green eyes or brown eyes? It's irrelevant, right? That's how I feel about gender. The heart and soul is the same.'

'Exactly,' says Huw. 'Hey, wanna go in the steam tent?'

We pick our way out of the hot tub and shiver over to the steam tent, a large contraption made of thick clear plastic draped over a metal frame. The setup here is similar to the hot tub, water passing through a heat exchange over a fire, but the fire runs a bit hotter to turn the water into steam. Quite often they hang a eucalyptus branch over the inlet nozzle, which makes the steam smell lovely. You can go around the back of the tent and throw a log on the fire if you want it hotter, or let the fire run down to cool it off. All sorts of random acts of creativity happen in here, from tonal chanting to massage circles. After dark, it functions partly as a gay men's pick up zone, and it slowly dawns on me that this might be what Huw is doing here.

Huw and I sit on one of the benches. The steam is thicker towards the top of the tent, so we reach up with our arms and wave it down over our bodies, in a move absolutely characteristic of the steam tent at HipHaven.

Someone walks past the outside of the tent. 'Want some more steam?' he yells.

'Yes!!!' we all chorus. We hear him go around the back of the tent and throw a log on the fire. A minute later, the inlet tube starts to hiss, and pulses of thick steam come into the tent. A cheer goes up. I can no longer see anyone but Huw.

'There were some things I've never done with a man, and last year I was doing one of them in here and our mate Mark walked in. He said to Fran it was a bit of a shock. I just feel like a freak.'

'Oh,' I say, surprised that the twirler gang is at all homophobic. I want to give Huw advice on coming out, to be brave and tell everyone, but I know from experience how difficult that could be. 'Well, maybe your next partner won't be female.'

'Maybe not,' he says.

At this point, another guy called Nick cuts in, and joins our conversation, and Huw flirts with Nick and Nick flirts with me, and I go outside because I am getting overly hot, and Nick comes as well. We stand around the fire and he massages my shoulders and stares at me intensely and told me he isn't real and comes from beyond this Earth, from the Great Field. I let him know that I'm not up for sex, and he says that's fine, and eventually the gentle tiredness of the night sets in and we reclothe ourselves. He has only brought a towel and it is cold, particularly after the steam tent and the fire, so he goes home in his towel and my arm warmers. 'I'm cold all over, but with very warm wrists,' he says as we part.

I walk to the market, to look at the swirling lights. There is a lot of sound and a lot of noise and a lot of people and I am a bit dehydrated and the thought of going home crosses my mind. I'm pretty sure there are some mates in the large swirl of people around the fire, but right now all sounds are a little bit too much. If my friend Rose is here, she may have parked her van where she's parked it before.

She is a one of the best people to be with when you are feeling quiet.

I walk disjointed, discoloured past the back of the market. There's a row of lighted marquees and they are full of blobs made where the clothes press against the nylon walls. This is how capitalism looks to a non-consumer, I think. Ten generators set up a loud drone and belch smoke into the air. It doesn't look nice, it doesn't smell nice, it doesn't sound nice. I know that if I were to push between the marquees the market would be attractively lighted, brightly coloured, filled with the distant sounds of the drumming. Sights to suck at the money in my bag. But back here, nothing is for sale. So many get the raw end of the market, I think. The factory workers in Taiwan, making stuff they could never buy. The fisherpeople scavenging the last of the fish from their ancestral ocean to feed greedy people out of tins. To my right is the back of the market, to my left the sacred ground marked off by our indigenous elders. Of course it is, of course it is.

The trees sit in the drone and the stink, shivering their leaves at the moon. I walk past out on to the plain, where a desolate wasteland of tents and cars has sprung up. In the daytime there's no shade out here, no ground cover. There's no talking, no people. It's silent. Everyone has come here to set up, leave and party. I walk to the left where the green river bends back around to greet us. My friend Rose has her camp on the lip of the cut bank, under a tree. I knock on the metal skin of her van, say 'Rose' softly.

She is gone.

SATURDAY

Mother

I wake early, having had a good night's sleep on my wonderful airbed. Chris isn't awake yet, so I sit in the sun eating grapes, sharing them with Ron, another early riser — and if you think this is going to lead to an affair, hands brushing over the luscious fruit and so on, you can think again. It's the last thing I have in mind, and I expect the same goes for Ron, who does not seem in the least amorous. For a start I have no intention of being faithless to my poor dear abandoned husband (who like Laura thinks I'm utterly mad to come here), and besides, the practicalities doom any romance. Two won't fit in Ron's coffin, and I'm not going to endanger my precious airbed by any sexual cavortings on it. And there's no way I'm going to roll about on the ground. Strained muscles would be the least of it.

Ron gets out his flute and Jethro Tull, and competes with the birds. The sun rises in the sky, sunbeams slanting through the trees. It's very peaceful: I had no idea that a hippie festival would be so tranquil. I had imagined it was all go, all music, dancing, drums, shouting, steam baths, hot tubs, rolling in mud and so on. From the wisp of noise that defeated my ear plugs it was like that till about 3 am, and now everyone's sleeping it off. Though someone, somewhere, is playing a drum. Throughout the whole of HipHaven, every single day, without a second off, someone, somewhere, is playing a drum.

I go to the long drops. In the queue I'm standing beside a very alternative-looking woman — nude, with exciting body paint and bright green hair. I can't resist it. I start chatting, then ask, 'What's your job, back home?'

'I work for Telstra. Customer relations.'

Whatever would her office colleagues say if they saw her now? I mentally wash her, clothe her in a neat uniform, undye her hair and yes, she could be young woman behind the desk answering queries politely and helpfully. I suppose.

It's my turn and in I go, musing. I'm a bit startled to see everything in the little annexe as spruce as can be. We've been here three days, and the loos aren't smelly — well, not very — and they're clean, and there are supplies of sawdust and toilet paper.

I come out, still musing. At the taps there is a young man with thick black long dreadlocks in bright orange happy pants, very earnestly and assiduously cleaning his teeth. I walk back to the camp, musing some more.

Chris is up, busy with the kettle. 'Chris', I say, slightly hesitantly as I don't want to criticise HipHaven — or say anything she might construe as criticism — 'are there any ferals here?'

'No', she says, pouring water in.

'Unemployed?'

'No, they can't afford it. It's $100 registration, which is fine if you're employed but too much if you're not. Then there's the petrol to get here, and the camping gear.'

I think of the four-wheel drives in the car park, people's jobs, the names I've heard, the tidiness, that young man so carefully cleaning his teeth the way his mum taught him. 'In fact, this is almost entirely middle-class. Not only that, it's pretty Anglo. Not many people of different races that I've seen.'

'Yes.'

'People in their twenties to forties, mostly. Having a holiday, drugs, nudity, letting their hair down, being idealistic, being nice to each other, doing what they like. Only in a responsible manner', I add, thinking of the lack of rubbish, the politeness in the queues. 'And very well-run', thinking of the continual supplies of toilet paper.

'Oh yes. The committee's good at it. They've been doing it for years. They have a team of vollies — volunteers — and they come here and get set up, and teams of people keep things clean and everything. It looks spontaneous, but it's really carefully planned. The vollies get to park right beside the tents, so they're happy.'

I had imagined HipHaven would be elderly ex-hippies my age, reliving their youth. But these people are much younger and quite different. They've still got the peace-and-love of traditional hippies, the tolerance and, of course, the clothes. Or lack of them. It's all extremely interesting. And if it had been elderly ex-hippies, I'd be sick to death of them by now. This lot are far more livable with.

The kettle's boiling, and Chris makes tea. Ron wanders off in his poncho, and we have breakfast. The bread is getting a bit stale, so Chris makes French toast with honey. Absolutely delicious, just scrumptious, couldn't get anything better anywhere, I tell her. The Paris Ritz — forget it. Andy emerges and looks longingly at the toast, but by this time we're nearly finished and I can't bear to give up my last delicious sliver. I tell myself I don't like to offer my already-bitten piece to a non-blood relation, a hygienic American. He accepts grapes happily.

We ask Andy the usual questions, where he's from, what he does. He sings the praise of his father — who turns out to be his stepfather, really — so wise, so supportive, such a great man. Nothing much about Mom. Andy's a really engaging young man, so nice, such a lovely smile, any mother's dream, you'd think. He's Jewish, he tells us, and he and Mom lived in Israel with his biological father till that broke up, and his mother remarried and moved back to America. 'Some people find stepfathers hard, he says. 'But mine was wonderful. Everything a father should be.'

'No problem avoiding pork and bacon here', I say.

He laughs. 'No, not much. I'm not really observant, but I did like living in Israel.' We chat about Israel, which Chris and I don't know much about. It's so enjoyable, sitting in the sun, interesting talk, no rush to do anything.

Andy's suddenly up and off, just as I'm saying we should get a photo. We look around for someone to take it. A man is walking along the path and Chris calls him over. 'Can you take a photo of us?' We realise too late, it's the sleazy old cadaver who annoyed Sue yesterday. Today's T-shirt is maroon and has a sunrise and the words 'Stop acting so small. You are the universe in ecstatic motion'. But we smile, and he takes a couple of photos of us having breakfast. He's pressed the wrong bit, it turns out, and no photos eventuate, but I don't mind as I don't want a photo taken by him.

'Now for a group hug!' he cries, so I hug him just enough to be respectable while he nearly throttles me. He sees a young naked woman walking along the path, gorgeous in the way of young women. 'Come and have a hug', he calls, and he embraces her very thoroughly indeed. She smiles as they break apart. 'That was a lovely hug', she says kindly.

'Am I right in thinking that was sleazy?' I ask Chris as soon as they're out of earshot.

'Yes, you sure are', she says vehemently. 'They're a problem, these old men.' Chris was once involved with the HipHaven administration and even thought of going on the committee, but it was too much dominated by old men, she says, with women just the ones who obeyed. 'They do what they can to keep them in check, but ...'

'Could that young woman have refused a hug?'

'Yes, she could say, "Not just now" or "I don't hug", but young women are people-pleasers. In ten years she might tell him to get lost.'

Chris makes another cup of tea. 'I'm impressed with how well everything's run here', I tell her. 'Look how quickly they dug a drainage trench when one of the taps was making a mud puddle.'

'They have a roster of volunteers', she says. 'You're meant to do two hours each. We'd better put ourselves down for First Aid.'

'I don't know much about First Aid. It's thirty years since I did a First Aid course.'

'Doesn't matter, it's mainly giving out bandaids. And better than cleaning toilets.'

Chris would love to go to the cuddle puddle, where you get in a puddle with a lot of other people, possibly naked, and everyone cuddles each other. I know she'd love me to do it but I just can't. I'm not a natural cuddler with people I don't know. Hugs yes, but ... She's so lovely, Chris, she doesn't even suggest it. We decide we should go to workshops, so we stroll to the enormous series of blackboards where people write down the workshops they want to run. This festival started out celebrating alternate lifestyles, and there's still a strong element of learning. Dozens of workshops are available. I might go to Spiritual Permaculture. (I can't imagine this. Isn't Permaculture about growing useful plants like almonds and broccoli instead of useless roses? Where does the spiritual bit come in? But perhaps everything's spiritual, really.) Tantric cooking (divorce if I went home and started tantric cooking, whatever it is). Astrology (appalling superstition! My opinion of astrology is summed up in a *Punch* cartoon showing a news item: 'The science of Astrology took a giant leap forward today when, as predicted, everyone born under the sign of Scorpio was run over by an egg-lorry'). Meditation (no! I can't bear it, so boring). Yoga (better, but I've done it). Aha — here's just what I need. Posture Exercises. I ditch Spiritual Permaculture and go to find it. I'm a bit early and sit on a tree trunk waiting, listening to what passers-by are saying. This is always fascinating at HipHaven.

'I've just had a massage. The man said he came from beyond the stars, and he isn't really here at all.'

'Off the planet!' They walk on.

A man in tights depicting all the muscles of the leg, very realistically. I'm gripped, yearning for a pair. He's telling a friend about — business? yoga? banking?

'I tell them to get out of the old profit and loss model and into the new flow of energy.'

Now the posture class is ready. A large tarpaulin, a carpet, cushions, benches. A marvellous young woman who works in this area gives us an excellent talk on the topic. I'm really glad to have this practical knowledge. Thanks, HipHaven.

There's one HipHaven moment though. The discussion veers to sitting.

'When I go to the toilet, I like to squat on a bucket', said one woman. 'It's more natural, and women are more in contact with the earth. I have a bucket in my bathroom.'

People who go to a workshop on Posture rather than Spiritual Permaculture are from the conservative end of the HipHaven spectrum. There is total silence.

Daughter

I'm in the queue at the chai tent when I see Pearl and Jessie. Pearl is a beautiful woman with deep brown eyes and a big smile. Of all the people I know, she seems to take stuff in her stride. She's been woven into the fabric of HipHaven for years, as a nurse with the first aid crew and also as part of the Sydney crew, who are a tight-knit sector of the festival.

It's through Pearl that I hear the first aid gossip, which is interesting. Several times they've airlifted people to hospital and I didn't ever hear the helicopter. Once a kid swallowed a bee and got stung in the throat. He survived, and the hospital staff praised the festival crew for their quick action. There's a doctor always present and the crew wear walkie talkies when they're not at the first aid station. I've been sitting at the chai tent with Pearl when the radio has squawked: 'PearlPearlPearl!' and she's gone off to deal with something. The crew are tight-lipped about what happens to who, though. I mean sure, I know a kid swallowed a bee, but I never knew the kid's name.

On the way into the festival, Greg and another first aider were standing by an ambo as someone was getting stretchered in, presumably on their way to hospital.

'Hi Greg,' I said, with a wave out the car window.

'Go in the gate,' he said, pointing firmly. You get that way if you've been dealing with people for a long time. You're so used to stopping people gawking at someone in a stretcher, you'll shoo away your mates.

One year, we had a fire where a campstove exploded. The whole site ran to put the fire out. Then there were so many people around, it was hard to get the truck through to actually put the fire out. We have a fire truck onsite, by the way. Then they had to get volunteers holding everyone else back out of the way.

So the first aid crew don't let any hint of an emergency get to the ears of the general festival population, unless it directly affects them. Pandemonium is seen as highly counterproductive. I like to tap into what's going on, though, so I hang out with first aiders and Pearl and catch a limited version of the gossip as it goes flying by.

Pearl is also one of those people whose life is an advertisement for motherhood. She loves her kids, and genuinely says stuff like, 'Well, the best flatmates are your kids, because even when they're yelling at you, you're thinking, "look how great your language skills are!" I know a fair few mums, and most of them don't think that when their kids are yelling at them.

Greg rolls up. 'I didn't know you two knew each other!'

'Yup!' beams Pearl. 'We're BFFFFs!'

'What does that even stand for?' asks Greg.

'Ummm.' We look at each other.

'Best friend friend friend friend friends?'

'Best friends of fortune and fried feral ... fecklessness?'

When we look around, Greg has left.

The other thing about Pearl is that she and I have no conversational boundaries whatsoever, beyond the first aid stuff. I always need at least one friend like her in my life, and preferably ten or more. You can stroll up to Pearl, having not seen her for a year or more (she lives in Sydney) and say, 'So, I pulled this weird thing out of my nose this morning,' and she'll say, 'Yeah?' and maybe chime in with a nose story of her own, usually even more revolting, and starting with the words, 'I had a patient once ...'

There's no 'ew' or 'shoosh' from Pearl. It is probably related to the fact that she was a nurse and then a midwife, and now works in the nurses' union. On maternity leave. Her daughter Jessie is the blondest toddler ever. Now and again, I meet a kid that doesn't like me, and she's one of them. Has been ever since she was a tiny baby. But I live a long way away, and the main person Jessie needs to like isn't me, it's Pearl and she loves her. I remember when Jessie was a few weeks old, Pearl wasn't wiped out or grumpy at all. She was fascinated to have gone through labour recently. 'Labour's a metaphor for everything for me right now,' she said. 'You just have to surrender to it.'

'Dude,' I said. 'You're evil. No one looks this good six weeks after having a baby. No one. You make new parenting look unrealistic. I know you haven't had any sleep.'

'Well, it's cool,' she said, brightly. 'Look how amazing she is!'

Anyway, that was two years ago and now Jessie is walking and climbing and getting smeared with mud.

'How much maternity leave have you got left?' I ask Pearl. She used to love her job, pre Jessie.

'Well, that's the thing!' Pearl wails. 'I have to go back to work and leave JessieBear in childcare! I have no idea how I'm going to do that! I love her too much!'

'Mate,' I say. 'You're the most superamazing hot chick in the world and you'll know what to do. But it must be really hard.'

'I went to the childcare centre and they were really nice and lovely and everything, but I started crying four seconds after I went in there! Usually the kids cry, not the parents! I mean, they were all very understanding, but ...'

'Oh honey,' we hug. I think about how Pearl's mum was a heroin addict and I have absolutely no idea how Pearl turned out so well. None.

'I don't understand how you turned out so well when your mum was a heroin addict,' I say. 'You're a miracle!' Like I said, we don't filter much.

'Thanks, I know. I'm amazing.' She smiles like a movie star in a paid interview.

'So, how are the other kids, they're not here?'

'No, they're with their dad this weekend. It's just me and Jessie. Anyway, how are things with you?'

'My mum came! I can't believe she trusted me enough to come up here! In the mornings, we have tea!'

'Aw,' says Pearl. 'You're so lucky.'

Her mum is dead, of course.

Mother

After lunch Chris tells me, to my surprise, that she'll come with me to the workshop on Making a Twine Water-bottle Carrier. It's at the craft café, and is likely to be endearingly amateur.

Daughter

It dawns on me that instead of Mum coming to do stuff I like, I can go and do stuff she likes. I feel embarrassed that I didn't think of this sooner. Before we leave, I turn to Mum. 'Did you put on sunscreen? Do you know the way back? Have you filled your water bottle?' I ask.

'This is such a role reversal,' she says, laughing. We walk to the workshop in the sunny morning, hand in hand. We're late, because I was fiddling around and didn't leave enough time, but it doesn't matter because the woman who is supposed to be running the workshop went shopping in town and nobody can predict how long she'll be. Could be days.

Mother

Some of the craft people look for twine. There's not enough, so they get wool. Someone else starts telling us what to do. 'Stretch out your arms. You need twelve lengths of twine round your hands.' That takes a while, organising people to get twine, finding someone to wind it round people's hands, losing count and having to work out twelve lengths again, finding scissors and cutting the twine, sorting out the knots the twine gets itself into, but eventually everyone is sitting with their twine (or wool). Then the substitute lecturer arrives, charmingly apologetic. Another lovely young woman. They're all lovely young women, so enthusiastic, so attractive, so kind and generous.

Daughter

The new craft woman seems a little lost with the crowd, which is big, ignorant and collectively stoned. You might think craft is a jolly good exercise for people off their chops but I'm here to tell you it isn't. It is a muddle. The string is muddled and the people are muddled and the co-ordinator is a little thrown. I ended up taking deep breaths.

Mother

First she tells us all to make a knot in our twelve strands, about 10 cm from the end. This is a bit challenging. Teaching always is: you think you're explaining but there's always someone who doesn't understand. So some people make their knot in the wrong place and have to be told what to do by their neighbours. Then they struggle to undo the first knot, and their twine gets tangled. Chris is bored and starts doing something with the wool around her toes.

Daughter

So I sit at my place in the circle with my twelve lengths of string, getting impatient and judging all the bloody stoner hippies for taking so long. One of the funny things about hippie encampments is that no-one thinks of themselves as an actual hippie. Nearly all the hippies I know, including me, get impatient at the other hippies and call them hippies as if we're not. Only we all are, really.

Then I breathe deep breaths and remember I'm here to be with Mum and spend quality time and look, haven't I got sunshine and peace and isn't this lovely really? But there's a section of my psyche that can't let go of the idea that we have a job to do, and that job is string water bottle holder making, and the bloody hippies are getting in the way of the task completion that would otherwise happen.

Mother

Finally everyone has now tied his, her or its (if transsexual, or is it intersexual? or intrasexual? But perhaps it's wrong to say its? I must ask Chris) knot, and it's time for the next step. We have to divide our twelve strands of wool into pairs, in order as they're round the edge of the knot. People get in a real muddle here.

I listen to what other people are saying. 'I've just run a workshop', my neighbour tells his friend. 'A floating tour of comfort — bring your own joint.' It's English, I suppose, but I have no idea what it means.

Daughter

Eventually, some instructions get issued and we duly follow them and then sit round waiting for the others to get round to not listening and having lengthy discussions about the whole thing.

Mother

Most haven't done any macrame before, it's clear. Then we make a knot in each pair, about 10 cm from the end. That's reasonably straightforward for most of us. But then we have to make another knot in a different pair, still keeping to the round-the-edge principle. This is a lot harder. It's easier if you do it on the bottle, I find. I get the hang of it quite fast.

Daughter

Mum catches on quickly and streaks to the lead with the innovative idea of tying the sides with the drink bottle in place. You'd have to be there to see how much better this is. I stick stubbornly to the recipe and frown my way through the project.

Mother

I finish my carrier, but most people haven't finished, and it's time for the next class with people arriving, and what with one thing and another, there's chaos.

Daughter

Glancing up, I see someone out the back in a classic craft outfit — track pants, boots, thick socks with the track pants tucked into them, a t-shirt and a bum bag. 'That's Sue,' says Mum. 'She runs the place.' With a bum bag like that, this is not a surprise. I'm not a feminine type of woman. I'm more the type of klutz who only ever gets told not to do things in crafty places like this ('Oh, just put it anywhere. Except there. Or there. Here, let me.'), so I'm looking at Sue with mild and thinly-disguised hostility. At the same time, I kind of wish she would take over our workshop and organise everybody. She's probably craft-workshopped out at this point, and likely to get more so over the weekend. Sue is talking to another woman, who is probably called Anne or Barbara, about craft-related issues. I can tell by the angle of their heads. Clearly, serious matters are being discussed. I can't hear what's being said but I wish I could, because it would be more interesting than waiting for forty people to finish a row of knots, while forty other people try to move them out of the way.

Mother

We're shunted off to the side, and Chris and I go back to the tent for a cup of tea (we don't think we'll stay for Advanced Crochet). I'm extremely proud of my finished product. I have to boast to someone. 'Look', I say to Ron, with great satisfaction. 'Look what I made. A water-bottle carrier.'

He looks taken aback, with one of those thought bubbles coming from his head: how on earth can I answer this inane remark? 'Ah, very nice', he thinks up. Poor man. I'm being ridiculous, carrying on in this way, like a six year old — but that's what it's like, being back at school, showing your mother your gold star for colouring in the map neatly.

Mother

Well, for goodness sake. Chris tells me everyone was stoned at the workshop. I had no idea. It's just what I was expecting a macrame workshop to be — a shambles. And she's critical of the way it was run! I'm even more surprised. I, Sally, not usually blessed with much patience (I can just imagine all my friends laughing and digging each other in the ribs at this statement), just let it all flow over me while she was getting cross. But she never was one for craft. I never got far trying to teach her anything, recreate my happy days at Mum's side while she guided my hesitant fingers into their first knitting stitches. Never mind. Chris loved learning to cook, standing on a chair in the kitchen mixing eggs till it's all a yellow colour darling, just like I used to.

My own dear mother was a wonderful teacher, so patient and encouraging. Faced with burnt cakes, collapsed-in-the-middle sponges, lumpy custard, whatever, she always had a cure and praise. 'Just cut the burnt bits off and ice it all over — it'll taste delicious.' 'Fill the centre with cream and jam. No one will know.' 'Strain it and it will be lovely.' And it was. I'd bring the cake to afternoon tea and they'd all fall on it with praise — no problem, our family always fell on cake with praise. It had to be pretty thoroughly burnt to get the thumbs down. And I knew perfectly well that never even by the merest hint would Mum give our secret away.

I'm quite proud of myself, being so patient. I wouldn't be at home. If some historical activity was such chaos, I'd be tapping my feet and pursing my lips with the worst of them. But here, time doesn't matter. Learning to make a water bottle carrier or not doesn't matter. What does matter is being calm and relaxed and peaceful and nice to everyone all around. I feel I'm getting the hang of it quite well.

Our third workshop for the day is Non-Violent Forest Protest. We've both had experience here. Well, I've been to a number of protests, and Chris started going to them in her pram. A couple of years ago she was arrested for protesting against a fast food outlet being built in her Melbourne suburb, because she was sitting on the roof of the existing building on the site so it couldn't be demolished. I got that phone call parents dread. 'Mum, I've been arrested.' I was behind her all the way, went to Melbourne for the court case, offered financial support, cheered with her when the case was abandoned. Well, who took her to her first protest? They built the outlet anyway, but it isn't doing very well. This is a green, alternative suburb in the hills, and the locals don't approve of fast food.

We find the Protest workshop, with a bit of difficulty. First we go to an Anarchy one, then to Fire-twirling, and finally we run accidentally into Protest, next to a song and dance one so our workshop is a bit hard to hear. Protest is run by three activists, lovely and serious young people, and it's a group discussion. People say what protest techniques they've been involved with and the result, or what they've heard about, and everyone takes part. It's very interesting. Someone describes putting sugar in a printing press so the material comes out unusable. I don't like destructive things but that doesn't sound like a good argument, bit sentimental, so instead I think up: 'Isn't that a waste of resources?' They agree it is. The discussion continues. I feel I've done my bit today by HipHaven workshops, and I've enjoyed them.

I drift off into vague pondering. The song and dance people next door are really enjoying themselves. They're in a conga line now, leaping round happily. That girl's wearing a nice skirt, nice shade of green. The young man leading our discussion — what a pet. A lovely soft voice, gentle face, neat little man-kilt and dreadlocks. What must his mother think. I wonder how they make dreadlocks. With a crochet needle, Chris tells me later. It's quite difficult and time-consuming. I bet it is. And even harder to take them out. She once helped a friend take out dreadlocks. They looked up how to do it on the internet, and then put a whole bottle of conditioner in her hair, waited an hour and cut the dreadlocks five centimetres from her scalp. It took two people took an hour to comb out the ends of the dreadlocks, but the friend had a respectable amount of hair to wear into the office on Monday.

We go over time, everyone's enjoying the discussion so much. A man turns up to take the next workshop, on philosophy of some sort, but he has no takers. I feel sorry for him, and tell him six o'clock is too late, everyone's thinking of the evening ahead, not workshops. So he joins our talk as well. I don't think we come to any useful conclusion, but there you go. We've all had a good time.

What I'd really like now is a shower, but the only shower block has an enormous queue outside it, and they're all nude. So I go back to our camp, get a bowl of water and have what my grandmother used to call an APC, washing my armpits and crutch. (A brand of aspirin was called APC, so you could say 'I'm going to have an APC' and it sounded innocent.) It's not really satisfying, but it's better than nothing.

So why don't I want to go nude? I don't really care if people see me naked. At least, in theory I don't. Or perhaps I do. Chris and I used to go nude swimming at a secluded beach when she was a teenager, but that was twenty years ago, and I was twenty years younger, twenty years firmer, thinner and perkier. And the beach was secluded. I've seen a few older people nude here and really, it's not a good look. Very saggy and baggy, pendulous breasts, drooping bum, rolls of fat round the waist. It's OK for young ones in their thirties, even forties, fifties at a pinch, but sixties — clothes look better. But nobody cares, and why do I? I ponder this. Perhaps this is just vanity, but I've never felt as though I had anything much to be vain about.

It's nothing to do with sex. For all the nudity at HipHaven, any sex happens in seclusion — like Nimrod and Onyx's parents having a go in their tent the middle of the night. They've certainly earned it! In public there isn't even much snogging. The whole place is a peculiar mix of exhibitionism and prudishness. Later I ask Chris why the hessian doors of the long drops go right to the ground. If they were a bit shorter you could see if they were occupied or not. 'They did have them shorter', she says, 'but people complained. They didn't like their feet being seen while they were sitting there.' There's a urinal on one side of the long drop complex where men used to urinate openly, in view of the waiting queue for the seats. But then a modesty screen appears, so the queue can't see. More complaints, I suppose. Why bother, when the men are walking round naked? So we all have our hang-ups about something? Defecation remains a strictly private activity, I notice. On reflection I think that's a very good idea.

For a little break, I turn to another Agatha Christie. This one is *Murder at the Vicarage*. Wonderful! Colonel Protheroe found dead on the floor, with dozens of enemies, any one of whom could have done it. But only Miss Marple can find out the killer, since elderly women are much cleverer than trained police detectives, lawyers, doctors, husbands and all male authority figures. So satisfying. So unlike HipHaven, where enemies are unknown. Except among the fire-twirlers.

Chris arrives, and cooks a delicious mushroom carbonara, with spaghetti, cream, egg, silver beet, mushrooms and olives. Not exactly what charcoal burners ate after a hard day's work, if that's the meaning of carbonara, but just what we want today. HipHaven is vegetarian and we're eating vegetarian, not out of conviction or obedience, but because Chris says meat is what causes gastro when there's no refrigeration.

After dinner I wash up and we sit around and chat for a while. I tell Chris how unrealistic detective stories are, because murdered people have to have lots of enemies, real enemies who hate them enough to kill them. 'I don't know anyone who hates anyone else enough for murder,' I say, mentally reviewing my acquaintances. 'At least, I don't think I do. Perhaps at the university — but it hasn't happened even there. It could, I suppose. Murder in the Sociology Tearoom. How about that?'

'Motive?'

'Oh, lots. Giving a bad peer review. Challenging the Honours result of a favoured student. Leaving the light on in the photocopy room AGAIN. Criticising a paper the murderer gave. Hogging the chocolate biscuits. They can be terribly petty, academics, and also clever and inventive and often unscrupulous. I'm glad there don't seem to be any here.'

Chris talks me into going out. I don't suppose I can really justify sitting at home for another evening, even though the Colonel's body has just been discovered. Besides, I feel I'm getting the hang of HipHaven — I haven't counted the hours remaining for ages — so off we go.

Daughter

'Well, there's one thing you can't leave without trying, and that's a baked spud from Norton's,' I tell Mum. She looks a bit dubious — a baked spud is a baked spud, after all, and they're not that exciting. But, bless her, she comes over to Norton's, believing in me, or the festival, or something.

'Two spuds,' I say, 'and have you got any gluten free?'

'You'll have to take that up with Norton,' he says. Around the back of the stall are the usual collective of hardened urban activists. The rest of the festival defines cool in flowing trousers and raver shirts, but here the dress code is strictly modified op shop. Hands are calloused and hair is naturally matted rather than arrayed into dreadlocks. Tall Tom is back here, a feather earring in his ear, and Gem, a blonde woman with a weary look and a laugh like a cockatoo.

Norton is further back by the sacks of dahl and spices. A row of ropes and climbing equipment hang from a truck. Norton is a bear. He has a big black beard, twinkly blue eyes, a deep chest, blue shirt, greasy leather waistcoat, bandy legs and shearer's boots. He never changes, never ages. Part of the anarchist collective, he has a gravelly voice from too many joints and too much talking.

'Norton, have you got any gluten-free spuds?' I call among the chaos. His body language answers me: not now. He is tying a bandana around his head and flipping it back over his hair, putting a clean floral apron over his waistcoat. I go back to the counter and order two spuds with salad. I'll get the gluten free one when it's ready. We get salad in our bowls and Mum watches as the man prepares her spud. They only come one way. The potatoes are rolled in oil and flour and baked. Then the top of the spud is sliced off and the flesh is spooned out into a container of seeds, nuts and spices and mashed around a bit. A spoonful of hommus is placed in the cavity. A dash of teriyaki goes on the hommus, then two slices of avocado. The mashed potato is placed on top, then a slice of vinegary pickled beetroot. The top of the potato is replaced. A salt and seaweed combo is shaken on top. You eat it with your hands.

'Oh darling,' says Mum. 'This is absolutely delicious. The potato melts in your mouth. Skin so crisp.' I know what she's saying, but she is uncharacteristically rhapsodising with her mouth full.

'I helped him make them one New Year's Eve. You keep saying, "Do you want me to take them out yet?" And he says, "nnnnnnnnnnnnnooooooooooooo!" He won't let you take them out until they're dark brown, almost burned,' I say. 'That's the secret.' Only as I later learn, it isn't.

Mum goes to look at the stalls, and I help out while I wait for Norton to get around to making a gluten-free batch of spuds. While I was sitting with Mum, I had a moment of concern: I saw Norton, in the course of his preparations, subtly pour wine from a cask into a bottle with a label that says apple and raspberry juice. It is a jarring moment. A normal drinker pours wine into a wineglass. A normal drinker who is camping pours it into an enamel mug. But a problem drinker pours it into a container meant for another red liquid. I wonder whether I should say something and decide against it. If he wants help, he'll ask for it. And in fact, another recovering alco is currently doing his dishes. I recognised Brent from our workshops. He's a big shavenheaded bruiser who's done time in Pentridge. Norton would probably relate more strongly to him than to me. However, I file away my suspicions in case Norton ever does ask.

Norton has disappeared behind the trailer and so I go to see Benny and ask how I can help and he gets me chopping kale and slicing avocado and pounding dried seaweed in a tiny rubbish mortar and pestle. That's typical of Norton's — blunt knives, clapped-out pots and pans, and the best damn spuds you've ever eaten in your life.

Norton comes out of the cool room, wiping his hands on his apron. 'Hey!' I say, going to hug him.

'You want to ask me something, don't you?' he asks.

I hang my head. 'Yep,' I say, 'Any chance of a gluten-free spud?'

'Rmpf,' he says. 'Tom, we'll wack on a batch of gluten-free ones, eh?'

Benny's given me the job of mashing the beans for the hommus. There's a big black pot of boiled chickpeas, fava beans and brown lentils in a mysterious but precise ratio. The metal masher is so ineffective it might have been made of tinfoil. After an hour of this and other jobs, a row of spuds emerge in the gluten-free tray. Tom nudges me. 'Your spud's ready.'

I put down the lemon I'm juicing with relief and skip over to the bench. Tom assembles me a spud and passes it over.

Oh. My. God. The skin is crispier than ever, the flesh creamier. Teriyaki sauce runs down my hand, circling my wrist. I am in heaven. Cool hommus, nutty potato. Oh God.

Once it's finished, I wash my hands and go to finish my job, making tomorrow's salad dressing, and as I'm pulverising garlic I glance sideways and see Norton basting the next round of spuds with a soft, white fat. Last time I helped, it was an olive oil/sunflower oil blend. This stuff looks almost like ... No, it can't be.

I add two tablespoons of mustard and the garlic to the dressing, give it a shake and stow it in the cool room. Then I go to say goodbye to Norton. 'What's that fat you're using, is it coconut oil?' It must be, or the vegans would rebel.

'It's heroin, not ice,' he growls, softly. I'm not at all sure what he means by this obscure metaphor. I can only assume he means it's a high quality, knockout ingredient instead of a rough, cheap high. I lean over the unlabelled tub of fat and sniff it.

'DUCK fat?' I ask, trying and failing to keep my voice down. Vegans and animal rights activists!

Norton winks at me. 'Those vegans keep coming back for more,' he says. 'If you look at it, spuds are only carbohydrate. What I'm giving them helps 'em out. Shiny skin, glossy hair.'

I walk away, trying not to chuckle. Not only is he feeding animal stuff to animal activists, he's giving them the most upper-class, French aristocracy-style meat product in the world. You're really a ratbag if you can piss off the most anarchic, state-smashing ratbags at the festival.

Mum and I reconvene and wander in the direction of the steam tent. Suddenly there are Adelaidies all around us, drunk as maggots. It's like being surrounded by cockatoos. 'Guys,' I say. 'Are you Happy Drunks?'

'Ahahahah yes!' yells Dana, oblivious to the sleeping people nearby. 'We're the happiest drunks! You can ask anyone. Just ask that guy over there. Hey mate! Mate! You know we're happy drunks, don't you mate?'

The man looks a bit sheepish, and then a delighted smile curves across his face. 'You're the happiest drunks! All my friends have always said so.'

'See?' says Dana. 'See?'

I feel an urge to move the party away from sleeping kids and people like me, who are allergic to noise once they've settled down for the night. 'Where are you going?' I ask.

'Oh, we're following you!' says Tam. 'And you're going to the steam tent. It'll help Sally's arthritis.'

'Actually, it would help with my arthritis,' says Mum. 'What do you think, Chris?'

I'm surprised. I'd given up going to the steam tent with Mum. 'Sure.'

I notice Nick from last night's steam tent adventure, passing us. 'Hey Nick!' I say. He turns and pauses a moment.

'Oh hey, from last night,' he says, giving me a hug.

'We're on our way to the steam tent,' I say. 'Come with us?'

He seems only too happy, and slings an arm around an Adelaidy as we head off. On the way to the tent, we also pick up Ron, who's walking slowly along alone and is pleased to be asked to join us.

Sue is sitting outside the team tent, having a deep and meaningful conversation with a group of young men. This, I think looking at her, is surely one of life's great achievements. Being able to do craft all day and talk to young men all night. I salute her as we walk past.

There is the usual stillness at the beach — a ring of naked people glowing orange around the fire, the soft, slow presence of the river, the glory of the stars and the ubiquitous ambience of someone sitting on the beach playing a guitar. I see Dave popping round the side of the tent to go and put more wood on. Mum and I pause and look around us, drinking in the peace and quiet. Behind us, the Adelaidies throw their clothes in a pile and stomp into the steam tent with various cacklings and goings on.

'It's so lovely,' says Mum.

'Peaceful,' I say. 'Come on, I'll show you where to put your things. Are you sure you want to do this?'

'Darling, I came here for an adventure and I love the Adelaidies, they're fun.'

We leave our clothes on a stump, which is handy for putting your shoes back on when you get dressed again. I see our neighbour Andy by the fire, talking to an attractive woman. He seems to have settled in. Mum seems to expand once she's got her clothes off. She's a nudist at heart. Nudism isn't anything sexual, it's a love of the feeling of the air against your skin and you can't begin to explain it to anyone who hasn't done it. I don't believe we humans are meant to be covered.

Mum holds my elbow and we walk towards the steam tent. It's glowing slightly in the darkness beyond and admitting little puffs of steam into the night air from a leak somewhere on its roof. I feel the crunch of heavy sand under my feet. The gum leaves overhead shiver in the breeze as we push aside the curtain and step into the steam.

So the first chamber is steamy but not hot. Nobody is in here and it's dark except for the light from the fire outside illuminating one wall. At the far end is another plastic curtain.

'Ready?' I ask Mum.

'Ready.'

I push the curtain aside and we enter the noise and steam. There are puddles on the floor that I don't like to think about (it gets swept and hosed out once a day) and we totter over to a bench. The Adelaidies are roaring drunk and Mum and I are trying not to slip over. Steam swirls around us and the other people are dark shapes against the walls.

'I'm releasing my endolphins!' shrieks Tam.

'Endorphins!' says Maggie.

'No, my endolphins! They're swimming away! In the steam!' She's adorable. All the Adelaidies cackle with laughter and I'm glad it's dark so I don't have to pretend to like her lame pun.

'You need a sense of porpoise!' says Maggie. More screeches. Wow.

'No whale to go but up!' says Tam.

'I'm loving this,' says Mum.

'We're loving you!' says Dana. 'Your first steam tent experience!'

'You're egg-sharkly who we wanted to see!' burbles Tam.

'You see, we'd wanted to invite you sooner,' says Maggie.

'Seaweed. That's actually pretty good!' I say.

Maggie grins. 'I'm special,' she says. 'Look, you pull the steam down from the roof, like this!' Mum stands beside her and she sweeps the steam down over Mum, who turns around to get warm. I take one of those mental photographs you take when something wonderful is happening.

Out of the corner of my eye, I see Huw and some big guy. They seem close, so I decide to leave them to it.

Ron is standing alone, and I think I can also see my friend Vic in Henry's crowd. Henry's nasal voice penetrates the fug and I'm grateful I'm out of range and unable to distinguish any words.

The Adelaidies start singing and making up an entertaining dance (they're such good value) and I worry in case things are getting a little bit too extreme for Mum, but at that moment Sue enters the tent with a degree of verve. 'Sue,' I call. She comes over. 'Oh Sally,' she says to Mum, but also to everyone, 'There was a man who started a fight, and he wouldn't calm down and we all spoke to him, and in the end we had to call the police.'

'How dreadful!' says Mum. 'What happened to him?'

'They gave him a serious talking-to and he's gone back to his tent to sleep it off.'

'Sleep what off?'

'Ice,' Sue and the Adelaidies and I chorus. There's not a lot of ice at HipHaven, but it does exist. Of course, not everyone who takes it turns into a raving psychopath or no one would ever take it, but now and again someone does. The dramas can be predictable.

'Where was this?' asks Mum.

'Oh, just near the craft tent,' says Sue. 'We were packing up and he came over and got very belligerent.'

'Imagine bullying the craft tent,' says Dana. 'It's like vandalising an old age home. No offence.'

'None taken,' says Sue. 'I sat with him for fifteen minutes. We didn't realise he'd been in a fight until some people came over and told us. I swear, I don't believe in violence but in the end I just wanted to knock his damn block off.'

'I quite understand,' says Mum.

Huw and his manfriend are kissing each other spectacularly. Huw places his thumb on the man's lower lip and the man licks it. Beyond that I cannot see, because it is very dark and they are silhouettes against the walls, which are translucent and glowing faintly in the firelight. I'm glad Huw is getting some. I felt bad taking Nick from him yesterday, although I would have vastly preferred it if Nick had stayed in the sauna. Still, it was his choice who he pursued. He picked the unenthusiastic woman over the excited man. You can only try.

Huw's manfriend is pretty much the opposite of who I would have picked out for him. He is burly, with brown eyes and a black beard and pudgy hands. He has an openness and a caringness about him, as if he is just about to go off and rescue a puppy. Only he isn't about to rescue a puppy, he is about to do things with Huw in the steam tent and I am about to look away and give them some respectful privacy. Huw's friend leans in and kisses him, so gently for such a big man, and so soft. A look passes between them that is so raw. They lean back and they are holding hands and looking optimistic. That's sweet.

I've been listening to this, but at the same time my temperature has been peaking.

'Mum, I'm getting a bit hot,' I say. 'Do you mind if I pop outside?'

'Of course, darling,' says Mum. 'I'll just be in here with Sue.'

'Thanks. I'll be by the fire, drying off.' As I leave, I see Ron wandering over to join Henry's circle. Why on earth you'd want to be in a group presided over by the world's most boring man is beyond me. He must be really lonely, or a glutton for punishment.

I nip through the chilly entry room and head outside.

Mother
Well, here I am. I can hardly believe it. In the steam tent. Enjoying it! Coping with being nude! Actually, like many things, once you take the first step it's amazing how quickly you get used to it. Besides, it's true that no one cares two hoots what I look like, so I don't either. At least, not much.

I think it's the Adelaidies, really. They're enjoying themselves so much, absolutely unashamed of anything, that I want to as well. And I don't want them to think I wouldn't. I'd hate them to go home saying, Did you see that Sally? Bit prim, wasn't she? So I'm nude.

It's so relaxing. I can feel my joints loving it, lapping up the wet warmth, lying back, putting up their feet, letting all the stress and pain ebb away. It is a bit hot, Chris is right — she always is — but it's worth it for that wonderful ebbing feeling. Sue and I chat idly about various craft things we've made. I waffle on about a magnificent orange and red spiral scarf a friend of Chris's knitted me. I feel on firm ground here, and it's a bit of a relief. Outside, I don't know anything really, have no idea when people are stoned or on ice, exactly what ice is, all that sort of thing. My last experience with any sort of drug was a magic mushroom omelette in Bali in 1976, and there wasn't much before it. A drag on a joint as it was passed round at uni parties and the hash cookie were about it. I don't mind being the innocent and therefore half-witted old lady, a bit like Miss Marple — it's an easy role to play — but it is nice change to know what you're talking about.

The Adelaidies are nearby, laughing and joking. Henry's monologue seems to have stopped, so even he's taken over by the luxurious warmth. It must have been like this at some eastern court or other, I muse to Sue. Warm, rich, opulent. At least, it would be if we had gold-embroidered cushions and hangings. We discuss how you'd embroider with gold. She has, of course. Someone, somewhere, in HipHaven has always done everything. And knows everything. Sue nudges me. 'I recognised what you were about to say the other day, about —' she looks around and lowers her voice theatrically '— removing the external layer from a furry feline friend.' We laugh, 'Thanks for your timely question that let me change the subject!' I say. 'What a friend in need you were that minute.'

Sue tells me of a few other clangers people have dropped over the years, some worse than mine. One elderly innocent referred to the nigger in the woodpile. Now that really is an old saying, but ...

Someone does something with a log of wood — Chris told me how they make steam, but I've forgotten the details — and the tent fills with thick, luscious, lovely steam, so solid you can almost hold it. I can't see a thing, but who cares. It's gaspingly hot now, and the odd person leaves, but they're just blurs in the steam.

It gets hotter and hotter, and my lungs are telling me that enough is enough. 'I think I'll go outside for a breather,' I tell Sue. I stumble outside and thankfully breathe in the cool night air. The stars are shining overhead, it's a wonderful evening, life is just lovely, isn't it?

Suddenly there's confusion in the tent. What's happening? People are milling round. 'A doctor!' shouts someone. 'How do we get a doctor?' 'Can anyone do CPR?' Someone must have been overcome in the steam tent. I hope it isn't one of the Adelaidies.

Sue comes out, looking horrified. 'Someone's dead!' she tells me.

'Not just overcome by the heat?' I ask, hopefully but idiotically.

'No, dead. Strangled. Murdered.'

There's silence.

'Who?' I ask. 'Do they know?' NOT CHRIS! flashes through my mind. Oh no, it's OK, she's outside. NOT THE ADELAIDIES!

'Henry. You know, that —' she pauses. He's dead, and she's looking for a kind word. 'Older man, the one with the grey ponytail.' Death must take away his irritating features, both in reality and in the way we talk of him.

'Strangled!'

The Adelaidies come out of the tent, full of exclamations. We hear that Henry had the marks of strangulation round his neck. Thumb marks. It's horrible. None of us liked him, but to die in such a way, on such a balmy evening ...

'I think I might leave', Sue says. 'I don't want to have anything to do with it. The police will be here soon.' We all agree.

Daughter

I'm crisping off by the fire when Mum comes out. I've been talking about music with Tom and Sue's handsome man and a couple of Italian backpackers. My hair is nearly dry when Mum comes out of the tent, looking highly relaxed. I have a moment of concern about whether she's drunk enough water when someone starts calling for First Aid. Dave materialises with a two-way radio, and in less than a minute, Pearl comes out of the darkness and plunges into the steam tent. A few minutes later, other first aiders emerge. I hear that the ambulance is on its way. The first aiders and some others are forming a guard around the steam tent and Dave has disconnected the inlet hose and opened the doors, so the tent is now cold and lit from within by torches.

Mum and I sneak over to the stump without being told off, and retrieve our clothes. We dress in silence. I look over at the tent, where everything seems to be under control. In spite of my wonderful bandaid-applying skills, I don't think I could add much to the situation besides getting in the way. Sometimes the most helpful thing you can do is to leave, and thin out the crowd.

'I can't believe he's dead,' says Mum.

'Maybe they can revive him?' I ask. Sue snorts, not unkindly.

'Vale, Henry,' says Tom, behind us.

'I wonder if he has any family?' asks Nick.

We all look at one another. It's hard to imagine Henry having any family that didn't despair of him and end all contact.

'Let's go home, darling,' says Mum. We limp off into the undergrowth, feeling silent and hollow. As I lie down in bed, I don't think I'll ever get to sleep, but quite quickly I do.

Lying awake that night, a horrible suspicion clutches my heart. Henry was in the steam tent with Huw. If he was in and out that evening, he may have seen Huw experimenting with his sexuality. Henry's sense of social appropriateness might not extend as far as shutting up discreetly about what he had seen. I'm aghast. Huw wouldn't kill anyone to protect his sexual identity. Would he? Would he. I know him. But in one way or another, I knew them all. None of them would kill a person, not even Henry, not even when he was annoying and inappropriate and loud and predatory. Surely.

SUNDAY

Daughter

Morning is a special time of day. First I become aware of the hard ground beneath me. Then I open my eyes and watch the buttermilk-coloured walls of my tent move in and out in the gentle breeze. It's like the tent is breathing. Then I remember Henry being dead, and the whole disaster comes back. The sun is shining through the nylon walls in tiny pinpricks of light and I am alive and Henry, who was just annoying me yesterday, is not. I can't believe it. Of all the people, surely that randy old goat was going to live forever.

Sounds filter through the tent and eventually the pressure on my bladder increases and I go out to the loo. I come back to find Mum looking lovely in an orange top and gold scarf, talking to Ron. I fill the kettle as far as it will go. This situation calls for serious tea. Unbelievably, the child with the bicycle bell is still at it, as if nothing has changed. I feel relived for a moment that the murder was Henry and not little Onyx, or Mum would be the number one suspect. Then I realise that she was in the steam tent at the time of the murder, so she will be a suspect. I put that thought in the 'things to think about once I've had a cup of tea' file, and carry on as if it hadn't been thought at all.

I get two mugs and a spoon from the stump, and the tea out of the provisions crate. Ron wanders off for a moment. 'Mum,' I say.

I stand and we hug each other. We both cry. I'd been holding it in. Mum's the best hugger. 'It's awful,' I say. 'I feel bad because I didn't like him.

'Don't feel bad, darling', says Mum. 'Nobody liked him. He was a frightful pain in the neck, but he didn't deserve to die. You don't have to like everybody. It doesn't make you a bad person.'

And that is the real advantage of bringing your mum to a festival. She's the best at crisis support. What would I have done if she hadn't been here?

'If only I'd gone and spoken to him. I was avoiding him.' I seem to be going into irrational blather mode. 'I could have stopped it. I could have looked after him.'

The kettle is boiling, so I go over and add three teaspoons of tea, taking the opportunity to blow my nose and wipe my eyes, using the hankie that resides in the tent.

'Now darling,' says Mum as I hand her her mug, 'What exactly would you have done for him? Stood by his side day and night in case someone wanted to murder him? He was murdered because no one could see anything in there. The murderer made sure nobody could see it happening. So it's absolutely not your ...'

'Good morning ladies.' I turn around. A man in uniform is standing by Mum's tent. A policeman, big and chubby with sandy hair. Recently shaved and smelling like cleanness. The man looks over at Mum. 'Sally Alexander?' He asks.

'Yes,' she says.

'I'd like a word, if you don't mind.'

'Certainly.'

'Would you like a seat?' I ask, standing, awkwardly. Should I offer him some tea?

'No, thank you. Would you mind coming with me?' He turns to Mum.

There's something strange about watching your mum being led off by a policeman. I feel like yelling at him, 'You take care of her! She's a Tasmanian living treasure! And my Mum! The only mum at the festival!' I mean, she's not the only mum at the festival, but she's an emblem of hope to the many motherless festival-goers. I pour Ron some tea, and Andy, too, now that he's emerged. We sit without saying anything, waiting for Mum to come back.

I'm sitting glumly. Neither Andy or Ron are nature's conversationalists, and our conversation has petered out.

I know everyone said not to stress about Henry, but two thoughts are acting like pincers. One, I'm quite glad he's gone because he was a pain, and two, that you shouldn't ever be glad, even a little bit, when someone's strangled to death in a late night steam tent.

Freshly Shaved Cop is bringing Mum back along the track and she's looking quite perky and chatting animatedly to him. He's got the look official people get when they're charmed in spite of themselves.

'Perhaps confessing is cathartic,' I think, then chide myself for joking about Mum being a murderer, which of course she isn't.

'Mum,' I say.

'Darling! They've got a van, and ...'

'Chris Alexander, please accompany me,' the cop cuts her off. Perhaps so we can't compare notes.

Waah! 'Me?'

There's cops and then there's cops. I've worked with them for a long time, and I know. You can't be angry with someone when they helpfully leave the milk out for you when you're making coffee. But I know the other side, as well.

Humans operate on a system of tribal markings, whether we admit it or not. If you think you're immune, imagine rocking up at a restaurant to find your friend is wearing double denim. At my old job, I looked in the mirror one day and realised I had the wrong hair for the office. I went to the hairdresser, said, 'Give me office hair,' and shut my eyes. Back in the office, people started being much nicer. But by that stage I was hating them for being so shallow, so I never found out if I could kick it in their group or not.

So the cops are bristling with their own tribal marking system, being neat and clean. Simon has a harshly trimmed mo and a short black haircut. Denis is very, very cleanshaven and has a short brown haircut. Their blue wool uniforms are wrinkle free and they have bulky black belts with things on them. Denis works out and is broad shouldered. His posture is exemplary. There's something deeply neutral about his attitude, like he's trying to say, 'I have no personality of my own, so please don't ask'. Simon, on the other hand, doesn't work out and slumps slightly. He has a friendly attitude, as if to say, 'You can trust me. Just do what I say and you'll be OK'. He has a bristling of thick but sparse hairs on his pudgy white arms, as if he couldn't quite wash all the Neanderthal off himself, not even with all the soaps, shampoos and deodorants that are gently perfuming the van.

I guess if they're looking at me, they're seeing someone scraggly, ill-kempt and defensive. Judging by the number of people who turned away or quietly melted into the scrub as we walked over here, I'd say I'm not the most defensive person on site. My hair is basically never brushed. I'm very freckly and I haven't had a proper wash in a week. I'm wearing a man's shirt with cut-off sleeves, a pair of poorly-fitting shorts that hang too low, and leopard print sandals. I look unreliable. And my attitude would probably read as, 'Last time I was in this situation, it didn't end well. So get this over with because I will never trust you.' Or maybe, 'I'm scared. Please hold me.' Or 'Fuck you, ignorant cop scum.' Depending on the perspective of the viewer. Which is Simon and Denis.

'Please state your name and address,' Denis says once he's got the recorder on in the van. Golly. I woke up this morning in a festival with my friends and relations and happiness, and now I'm in a grey police van with swivel chairs and computer screens. It looks like the van they would use to run an incident in the field. My brain doesn't quite cope with the fact that I'm now giving my name and address and stuff. It's suddenly very official.

I can see their name badges. White guys. Shane and Dale. Shane is the cop formerly known as Shaved Guy. Dale is quite handsome and doesn't say anything.

'What time did you go to the steam tent?' asks Shane.

'Well after dark,' I say, quite pleased with my ability to pinpoint a time in spite of being a hippie.

They sigh.

'And you had your mother with you?' continues Shane.

'Yup,' I say. 'We picked up Tom and the other Tom and the Adelaidies and Nick.' I decided to give them all the names, after some thought. I don't want them to accuse anyone falsely. But I feel that I owe it to Henry to try and get to the bottom of his murder. And I owe it to the community to not let someone that's murdered someone walk around and potentially murder someone else. If it's a serial killer, which is unlikely.

Some of my friends at this point would say that I should shut up and let the community sort its own problems out. But while I love my community, I don't have much faith in our ability to resolve interpersonal disputes. I've seen violent guys welcomed back to the mob with open arms, while their partners are shunned. More than once. Maybe if we had the best community minds sitting in council regularly. Maybe if we still had our nonviolent dispute resolution group running. But we don't. And they're not.

So I sell out, and name my buddies. It may be that someone gets needlessly accused. I'm worried.

The cops spend some time piecing together what I've actually said and they get annoyed that I don't know anyone's last name, unless they're my friends on Facebook (and even then it's quite likely to be Dreamweaver or Starblazer). We establish who, exactly, the Adelaidies are. Which Toms are which. They start looking quite tired and out of their depth. They're rural cops, with a very limited attention span for city people who come to parties.

I'm not so useful for the crime itself because I was outside, but on the other hand the people inside didn't see anything either. Also, I can confirm who was around the fire at the time of the murder and exclude quite a few people from the suspect list. Sometimes it's helpful to be Rabbit and know all the friends and relations. I add in a lot of annoying details like how nice the guitar was, and what the moon looked like. I can't help it. Intellectually I know they don't need those details, but you can't just walk out of a festival and into a van and switch off the festival part of your brain. It's still on.

'Look.' I say. 'I trust you to sort this out. We all do. This has been an enormous blow to everyone here. We sleep in tents. The walls are made out of nylon. Anyone with a knife could murder us. You need to work out who did this. We've got people who are mentally ill here who are getting well. We've got addicts getting clean. A lot of vulnerable people come here. We might look like rich Melbourne people to you, but they're not here. Rich Melbourne people don't drive five hours over Easter to live in the dirt and meditate. We're here because we need to be here. Please give us back our safety.'

Shane looks at me, measuredly. 'The locals are spooked too. They don't want violent crime in the area. They're spread out with their families. We promise you, we'll do all we can.' And then he shuts down again, and his official mask falls back down over his face.

They established the time I went home to bed, 'Quite late,' and they let me out to walk myself back to camp. I'm a little annoyed that they escorted Mum but not me. Am I not special enough?

Mother

Well. I thought admiring a crochet needle was the most unexpected thing I'd done at HipHaven, but here I am being interviewed by a policeman. I haven't had much to do with the police. I follow the officer, who looks about fourteen, to a tent which is marked with police signs.

We sit down. The officer turns on a tape recorder, asks me if I mind being taped. I wonder what would happen if I said yes. 'No, that's fine', I say, of course.

'I'm Sergeant White from the New South Wales police force', he starts. 'I'm enquiring into last night's fatality.

Now, madam, were you in or near the steam tent last night?'

I was brought up to obey the police and tell the truth. 'Yes, I was', I reply.

'At what time were you in or near the steam tent?'

'I don't know when I arrived, but I left at about eleven.'

'How do you know the time?'

'I looked at my watch when I left.'

'Ah, you wear a watch.' This is not as fatuous as my age group might think: many young people don't wear watches any more because they rely on their phones. I've had quite a few ask me the time at HipHaven.

'Yes, I do', I reply, showing him. He nods gravely.

'What time was it when you entered the tent?'

'I don't know', I say. 'After dinner some time, but I'm not sure.'

"What time did you have dinner?'

'About seven.'

'And how long did you spend in the tent?'

This is getting a bit hard. My memory's not what it was, and last night's events are hazy. Does it make me sound guilty? There's something about being interviewed by police that makes you feel as if you've committed a hundred crimes. I wonder what criminals feel like. Innocent? 'I don't know how long I was in the tent', I answer. 'An hour, perhaps.'

'How many people were in the tent?'

'About a dozen', I say. 'Or perhaps twenty, or even more. I don't really know — I wasn't noticing.'

'Come, madam, surely you can give me a more precise answer than that. It was only last night.'

'Yes, but I was just enjoying the steam. I wasn't looking at other people.'

He barely suppresses a sigh.

'And did you know any of the other people?'

'No.' I'm not going to dob anyone in. I can see the next question coming, about Chris, and try to head him off. 'It was very steamy and people were very hazy, so I wouldn't have recognised anyone. Besides, I hardly know anyone here.'

'Were you smoking drugs, madam?'

'No.' He looks hard at me, willing me to confess.

'Have you consumed any alcohol in the previous twenty-four hours?'

'No' — the whiskey has run out. Another hard look, as if to say: what are you doing at this festival, then? 'Really I didn't. I'm just here with my daughter to see what it's like.'

'Did you know the deceased, madam?'

'Not really, but he did take a photo of my daughter and me. But I didn't know him to speak to — except saying thanks, that sort of thing.'

'Did you see him in the steam tent?'

'Yes, before it got really steamy. He was further away, with a group of people, talking. I did notice that he stopped talking.' I realise, too late, that I shouldn't have admitted this. It doesn't help the enquiry at all, because of course —

'When was this, madam?'

'Look, I really don't know. It was before we left the tent — sorry, of course it was. I don't know how long before. Ten, fifteen minutes, maybe? But I'm only guessing.'

'What were you doing at the time?'

'Talking to Sue.'

'Who is Sue?'

'I don't know her other name. You might find her at the craft tent. Dark hair, perhaps in her forties. I think she comes from Melbourne.' I'm glad to be able to give Sue an alibi. And she can do it for me, I realise.

'Were you with your daughter, madam?'

Chris. I can't let them suspect Chris. 'No, she left the tent some time before. She was getting too hot.' But they might think she went round the back and strangled Henry! I can't think of anything else to say, to exonerate her.

'Thank you, madam, that will be all', he says. Phew. 'For now', he adds. 'Please do not leave the campsite.'

'We were planning to leave on Tuesday', I say. 'Is that all right?'

'Please inform the police of any movement on your part.'

'Yes, certainly, officer', I say meekly. 'By the way, I can remember one group who were in the tent. I don't know their individual names, but we called them the Adelaidies because they come from Adelaide. They were all far too drunk to be capable of strangling anyone. I'd swear black and blue to that.' There, my good deed for the day and perfectly truthful — and would I love to hear the police interview between the innocent young policeman and the Adelaidies! In the kindest, most voluble way, they'd eat him up and spit out the buttons.

Back at the tent I tell Chris all about it. I'm feeling funny. Upset, turned inside out. 'Chris', I say, 'I think I'll go to a workshop, to get away from all this police stuff. There's one on Tantric Cooking.'

'What's that?'

'I don't know. That's why I'm interested. I'll tell you. I might not try it on Dad.'

It turns out to be very restful. No one talks about the murder. It's not the sort of something-awful-has-happened-but-it's-so-overwhelming-I-can't-talk-about-it silence with everyone looking grim, like after the Port Arthur massacre, and it's not something-awful-has-happened-but-it's-best-not-to-say-anything, with those knowing sideways looks. It's just silence. I wonder if they even know about it. I remember Chris saying the camp authorities are good at hushing things up.

'Well', I say to Chris as I arrive for lunch, 'all food is sacred, and the act of eating is sacred, because it's charged with sacred energy, owing to being blessed. And you have to eat things in season, eat moderately and leave a quarter of your stomach empty.'

'That won't be hard', says the cook. 'We're running out of all sorts of things. Celery does tend to leave your stomach empty.'

'That's not the right attitude', I say, mock severe. 'You have to be spiritual. Contemplative, meditative, forget anything egoistic. And don't eat meat because it encourages rage and materialism.'

'I wonder how they know', says Chris. 'Do vegetarians never get road rage?'

'The gods probably calm them', I said. 'It was all very peaceful and pleasant and everyone was looking very receptive and nodding politely, but it's like all these things, based on what people think might be the case. Rubbish, as far as I'm concerned, like yoga people talking about energy running up and down your spine. Just a nice idea. I didn't give up Christianity to believe something else without any credible evidence.'

'What was the cooking like?'

'It was nice', I enthuse. 'The man was very charming, and he made a vegetable curry with a pinch of something I hadn't heard of and a pinch of something else, and it was delicious. We all got a spoonful on a leaf.'

'What sort of a leaf? A gum leaf? That's the only sort round here.'

'It looked more like banana.'

'They must have brought them in specially.'

'A lot of trouble. You'd think plates would be easier. Saucers. You can get them for next to nothing at op shops.'

Ron comes over. He's heard our desultory chatter.

'Tantric cooking sounds marvellous!' he says excitedly. 'Wonderful for my digestion. I tend to suffer from cramps after eating, and this sounds like the answer.'

'It might well be', I say in a general sort of way, wondering if he heard me call it rubbish.

'Well,' he starts, and continues, unfortunately, all about his cramps and how long after eating they start and how long they go on for. We give him some celery. It's probably good for cramps. Well, it must be good for something. I'm not really keen on celery. We never had to eat it as children because Dad didn't like it. 'If God wanted us to eat celery he'd have made us rabbits', he used to declaim. A pity it lasts so long in Chris's makeshift fridge.

I start to chop tomatoes for lunch, bending over on my chair to cut them on the ground. This does not encourage contemplation at all, in fact it encourages crossness owing to being uncomfortable, but grizzling won't get the baby washed or whatever the saying is, and on I chop, while Ron tells me what sorts of food give him cramps. I'm rather surprised that this pleasant flautist is quite so stomach-oriented, but we all have our foibles. When he pauses for breath, I break in.

'No one at the workshop mentioned the murder', I say to Chris. 'They didn't look as if they'd heard of it. You were in the steam tent too, Ron, weren't you — did you see or hear anything suspicious? I didn't', I add quickly in case he feels I'm insinuating anything.

'No', he says. 'No, I was just sitting there, not noticing anything.'

'We all were, I think', I say. 'No one was in a noticing frame of mind. I don't see how they're going to find out anything.'

Andy comes up. He's looking pale. Poor kid, it's probably the first time he's had anything to do with violent death. Well, it's the first time I have, come to that, but I've had more time to get used to the idea. About forty more years. Not to mention dozens of Agatha Christies. They're not the same as reality, but they do get you used to the concept.

'Are the police saying anything?' he asks worriedly.

'No, and I wonder if they ever will', I say. 'No one seems to have seen anything, so how can they tell? And really, Henry. Just the thought of that long grey ponytail makes any urge to unmask the villain fade away.' Oh dear, I think, not very HipHaven. 'Though of course it's very terrible', I add quickly.

'Do they keep on looking until they've found the killer or do they give up?' Andy asks.

'If it's obvious they're not going to find anything, they give up', said Ron. 'Waste of scarce resources to keep on looking. Throwing good money after bad.' Oh yes, I think, he knows, he's a public servant.

'My authority says every murderer makes one mistake', I say, 'but I think that's made up by crime novelists so that the murderer has to provide them with a clue. The murderer doesn't seem to have done so this time. No footprints or bloodstains, no blotters with the fatal letter visible back to front.'

'What's a blotter?' asks Andy.

That forty years leaves a huge gap, doesn't it. 'About a thousand years ago', I say, 'when I was a little girl in school uniform and plaits, we sat at desks in neat rows, and we had pens, like biros but with nibs on the end. You dipped it in ink — which the Ink Monitor made up with ink powder and water, and poured into inkwells, little containers on each desk. You wrote with the pen. Like dipping your finger in paint and writing with it. Then, because the ink stayed wet for a while, so it wouldn't run you had a bit of very absorbent paper called a blotter, and you blotted the ink with it. If your ink was wet, you got the mirror image of your writing on the blotter.'

Weird, isn't it. Something all my generation know, but kids have no idea. 'So I suppose if you wrote very fast with very runny ink, you'd get a fair bit of writing on your blotter, enough to tell the detective the vital clue about the time of the villain's visit.'

'Mum, you're so promising with your blowpipes and blotters,' says Chris, grinning, 'but no, no blotters. Remember about everyone being nude.' If Ron and Andy weren't there I'd tell her about female convicts smuggling contraband in their vaginas, but it might be a bit much for these innocent males. Besides, it would be hard walking normally with a blowpipe up your vagina. Mind you, would anyone notice in the steam tent?

'I think even Agatha would have trouble finding a clue in this murder', I say, handing round the delicious almond biscuits Chris bought for me. 'It seems to me it will fizzle out. Good.'

'Don't you want the murderer unmasked?' asks Ron, still the law-abiding public servant.

'I suppose so', says Chris.

'But not desperately, to be honest', I say. 'Not as desperately as I'd want to see a child murderer discovered. I'm not going to do anything active to promote it. Not that I'd know where to start.'

Daughter

'It couldn't be you,' says Mum, 'and I know it wasn't me, but who else was in the tent at the time of the murder?'

'Sue, the Adelaidies,' I say. Mum retrieves a notebook from inside her tent door. 'I know it wasn't Sue, I was talking to her the whole time,' she says.

'Henry ... It wasn't him, of course, and Frank and Vic, and two men I don't know, and people outside, anyone could have crept in, and it was dark.'

'You had another friend in there, didn't you, darling?'

'Oh yes, Huw, and what looked like a man-friend. If we know one of them didn't do it, we could be pretty certain the other one didn't, because they were together.'

'The man that runs the steam tent,' says Mum, abruptly. 'Dave.'

'Yes. He went around the back.'

'Good point. He was putting wood on the fire. That would be the pulse of steam that obscured the murder.'

'What about the people outside?' Mum asks.

'Andy, Frank, two backpackers, the guitarist and a bunch of people over at the volunteer hut.'

'Let's assume it wasn't them.'

'Mum, you may have written down the name of the murderer there,' I say. We both look down at the book.

Weird. There are too many names. I don't see how this will be useful. The police will have a list as well.

'Darling, we need to look at motives,' says Mum.

'With Henry, there is only one motive. Someone got annoyed.'

'I don't think being annoyed would lead anyone to murder him. It might have been something else.'

So we create another list, of people with a reason to kill Henry, and see if anyone overlaps.

There's Sue, of course, who can't stand him, but she has a good alibi.

The man on ice who'd been in the fight could have circled around and come and sneakily killed Henry in a homicidal rage. Unlikely.

Pretty much all the men could have had girlfriends, sisters or lovers who'd been sleazed onto by Henry. Actually, that could have been everyone.

The people in conversation with Henry could have been sick of his tedious monotone.

We realise we're grasping at straws. We need more information. Also, we're feeling a bit ghoulish with all this. Luckily, it's time for our first aid shift, and so I load us up with a tedious amount of sunscreen, water, lip balm and hats and we set off. I would be lying to you if I said it didn't cross my mind that we might be able to get some better-quality gossip at the first aid tent.

Mother

Late afternoon, Chris and I are on duty at first aid. You're meant to do two hours' of volunteering at HipHaven. A lot of people don't, but owing to being well brought up, we do. Anyway, it sounds interesting. Chris always puts herself down for the first aid tent, and by now she knows the ropes.

The tent is a huge dusty marquee with rooms along one side. They house the equipment, which someone shows us. There's a lot, including a defibrillator. The tent is staffed by a qualified doctor, a Leading Med person who's also qualified (a nurse, in this case), and four or five helpers who don't have to know anything, though it's useful if they do. This team can deal with almost all the problems, and if not they can call for an ambulance fast. Like all the organisation at HipHaven, it's well planned, well equipped and generally very impressive.

I'm a bit confused by the showing-round and instructions, and since there's hardly anyone wanting help, I decide to sweep. Like craft, it's something I know how to do. With all the dust at HipHaven the tent needs sweeping all the time. You finish and you start again, like painting the Sydney Harbour Bridge. I take pride in getting up every last particle. Then someone walks in and I do it again. No problem. I'm being useful.

Chris is in her element. Just about everyone at Hiphaven goes barefoot, and most of our customers have cut their feet. They're given a basin of warm water with disinfectant and soap. They soak their foot for a while, till it's looking cleaner, and the volunteer can pat the cut clean, dry it, and put on antiseptic cream and a bandaid. These people aren't badly hurt and they rather enjoy it. Everyone chats in a friendly way, sitting in a half-circle of plastic chairs having their feet washed and cared for.

There's also a free supply of bottled water, moisturiser, sunscreen and insect repellent (though, remarkably, there aren't any flying insects to sting you at HipHaven), and leaflets about health matters. People come up, and I direct them to the free table, or to the cut feet circle. Occasionally there's more. A woman has cut her finger quite badly severing a pumpkin. 'You'd think I'd know by now', she says sadly. The Leading Med treats her. A boy has a deepish cut on his foot, and he too gets the Leading Med.

With the free things there's a photocopied book, a history of the festival, one of those compilations of people's reminiscences. It's fascinating, though in the way of these things, all very positive, as though there have never been any problems. Photos of people laughing and smiling and having a good time. There's one frank entry. They asked a five-year-old girl what ideas she was taking home from the festival. 'Men look better with clothes on', she said.

Ha, childish wisdom! I go back to the sweeping. Another volunteer takes turns with me on the broom. I adore him. He's called Sam, in his forties with a huge grin and red spiky hair — natural red, not dyed. He's wearing black shorts and a plain grey T-shirt.

'Aren't your clothes a bit staid for HipHaven?' I ask, proud of my golden skirt.

'You should have seen me last night!' he chortles. 'Frilly spangled white tutu, dancing on the tables! And a red feather boa.'

'Fabulous!' I say in awe. 'How on earth did you get a red feather boa?'

'Bought it at one of the stalls' — the obvious answer.

'How energetic of you! I hope you didn't fall off', I say. 'The tables, I mean.'

'No worries', he says, 'When you're high you don't fall, and if you do you don't hurt yourself.' Well, that's a handy bit of knowledge.

Sam lowers his voice. 'Do you know anything about this murder? I've heard he was CIA.'

'I was in the steam tent, and I saw him, but I don't know anything', I say. 'It was so steamy, you couldn't see a thing. I don't know about the CIA. Are people really CIA or is it something they just say? What would a CIA agent be doing here?' I look round at the bush surrounding us.

'Having a weekend off, perhaps.'

'Yes, I suppose even CIA agents get free time. Perhaps someone's on to him, followed him and ... but it doesn't seem very likely.'

'Conspiracy theories are never likely. That's why people love them.'

'He was a very annoying man, but I don't know that it's enough of a motive. He was the one with the long grey ponytail.'

'Him!' says Sam. 'Him! The one who lectured me about being gay! Well! I'm not surprised someone bumped him off. Thought gay people were an abomination! Just as well I wasn't in the steam tent or I'd be Suspect No 1.'

'You wouldn't really, though', I say, looking at his kindly face, cross though it is just at the moment. 'Would you? Would you know how to strangle anyone? Would you really do it?'

'I don't suppose so', he admits, a trifle sadly. 'No, I don't know the finer points of strangling. You never see that close on TV. Anyway, they don't seem to actually strangle very often. Knife, yes. Bashing up. Poison even. Not strangling, though. You'd need an SAS person for that. I believe they learn it.'

'No one round here looks very SAS', I say, pointing to the cheerful crowd at the cut feet circle, the naked people walking past, laughing and chatting.

'Put them in army fatigues and give them a gun, and you'd never know them,' says Sam.

A girl comes in sobbing with a bad gash on her knee. 'Fell off a bike', she chokes out. Sam and I leap in to help — get the Leading Med, sit the girl down, get a basin of water, soothe and calm. Henry fades into the background.

Mother

After dinner, Chris goes off for the evening's activity, and I sit in my comfortable chair looking at the stars, thinking about her. She was the dearest little girl. Solemn, earnest, eager to please. She had seventeen months of being the only one, adored by both parents and four grandparents. Unless things have gone pear-shaped, all oldest kids have this wonderful period of being the centre of attention. What a pity we can't remember it — I was the oldest too. I wonder what sort of effect it has.

Chris was a dream child. Loved doing things with Mummy. Loved being read stories. Docile and reasonable. She didn't even do pesty things like I used to, climb into my parents' bed at some frightful hour of the morning, waving a book and crying out 'Wead! Wead!' (as my parents moaned to me later). Chris's love of literature showed only at civilised times. And she was at the forefront of all those milestones of childhood. She was saying three-word sentences by her first birthday. The usual time for this is the second birthday. Wow! You think you're such a brilliant mother. Then number two comes along and doesn't speak at all for ages and ages, until she brings out a perfect sentence. And after a while you realise it all comes out in the wash, they all end up much the same. But it's comforting at the time, having your first child do all the things she's meant to.

Ah, wonderful memories, but I have a reality check. A photo. In 1978 my first book was about to be published. A man came from the local paper to take a photo. In the paper appeared a head-and-shoulders of me, looking quite serene, holding up a book against a background of a bookcase, all fine. I bought the uncropped photo from the newspaper. There I am, looking quite serene, holding the book and so forth, but underneath this charming scene my heavily pregnant waistline billows out, and further down toddler Chris, standing in a rubble of toys, grabs my knees, her mouth open at full stretch, howling, given up to misery.

She ran away, like they all do. Several times, I think, but once I remember well. We were in the supermarket, and suddenly she wasn't there. I raced around with the baby and the groceries in the trolley, no Chris, raced outside, looked everywhere, and there she was, halfway up the fire escape on the outside of the building, a tiny little toddler figure. Someone must have kept an eye on the baby as I rushed up the steps after her. Then I had to go back inside, feeling like an idiot and, worse, a Bad Mother, and pay for the groceries.

But they grow up, thank goodness. She was the one who loved bushwalking. I've always loved bushwalking. Dad did too, and he took me with him from an early age. We lived at Oatlands till I was four, and I have a golden memory of walking by the lake through flowering yellow broom with Dad and the dog, a glossy black Labrador called Havoc. In the sunshine of course — golden memories are always in the sunshine. Dad and I were the keen walkers in the family, and later on Dad took me off for the day to national parks. A memorable walk was to Hartz Peak, a favourite destination, such an exciting rocky climb at the end. Mum had made us an egg-and-bacon pie for lunch. At about eleven o'clock, Dad said, 'I'm sick of carrying this pie. Let's eat it.' So we did. At eleven o'clock. If Mum had been there, we wouldn't have dreamt of eating it till proper lunch time. It was excitingly rebellious, doing things with Dad. My goodness, that's using the word 'rebellious' in an unusual context. If that's the most rebellious activity ... but Hobart wasn't a very rebellious place to grow up. Eating in the street in school uniform was about the worst sin we ever committed.

You like recreating things you enjoyed in your own childhood, and I took Chris on lots of walks — though we probably only ate lunch at lunch time. Hartz Peak, Mount Field, Cape Raoul — Hobart's so lucky, lots of wonderful day walks fairly close by. By the time she was about eight we walked at the same pace, and we'd have great days in the bush, talking endlessly about everything we could think of. We also loved swimming in the ocean, bodysurfing — Dad taught me to bodysurf too, and catch waves on an inflatable mat. I passed the lessons on to Chris. We had great times in the water.

Once, in her twenties, obviously being very brave and breaking bad news, Chris gathered up her strength and said, 'Mum, I'm bi'.

'Oh', I said, rather taken aback but not of course wanting to show it. 'Well, either way, I hope you find a nice partner.'

'Don't you mind?' she asked anxiously.

'No', I said, quite honestly. 'As long as you're happy, I don't care a bit.' You don't, as a parent, do you. As long as they're happy.

I don't want to suggest everything was always ideal. Of course it wasn't. We had our ups and downs like any other family, still do. There was a tough patch when Chris was fifteen or so — I remember that all too well. But she still liked bushwalking.

MONDAY

Mother

I'm woken by birdsong, and if there's a more beautiful way to be woken ... well, I suppose you could think of one (arms of ravishing lover) but this is pretty good. Onyx's parents seem to have forbidden the bicycle bell, in the interests of community life. I get out my last Agatha Christie. Another good one, *Cat Among the Pigeons*, death in a high-class girls' boarding school. It's an interesting background, though they never seem to do any lessons. Why are French mamselles always a figure of fun? I wonder. Not German teachers, or Maths. I read on, trying to get hints to help us through this similar situation — well, sort of similar. But an elderly spinster shot in the sports gymnasium at an exact time leaving bloodstains and other clues doesn't help me much.

I hear Chris stirring and get up. It's familiar now. Finding things in the tent, doing my hair by feel — and it feels pretty manky by now. I don't mind that there's no mirror. I'll be glad to have a shower tomorrow. Very, very glad. And get back to my own lovely bed, lovely husband, lovely armchair, lovely benches at waist level. Though I've enjoyed HipHaven. Well, a lot of it. Being with Chris, mostly.

The kettle's boiling, and Chris and I have tea. 'Chris', I say, 'we ought to go through all the suspects and look at them. I'm being Hercule. Or perhaps his half-witted hanger-on, the Doctor Watson man. You can be Hercule.'

'Right', she says. 'Start with me. I could have ducked round the back of the tent, I suppose, though it would have been hard to see. But that goes for everyone, really.'

'Motive?'

'I didn't like Henry. I've had mentally ill episodes, I could have snapped.'

'That goes for a fair few people here, I'd think', I say, horrified to hear Chris talking about mentally ill episodes in this frank and accepting way. But it's not the time or place to say anything. It never is, really, for a mother. 'You don't really sound very probable. If you'd murdered Henry, surely you'd have been more upset since, and you've been just as usual. I don't see how anyone could murder someone and not be upset.' I'm glad I thought of that one. I can't seriously picture Chris as a murderer.

'How about me? I was with Sue, but we were pretty dreamy, and either of us could have nipped out for a tick, found Henry, strangled him, and nipped back. Sue's a pretty strong feminist and she couldn't stand Henry.'

'Didn't you say you were both dreamy?'

'The murderer would only be pretending to be dreamy. Perhaps if you had murder in mind that would overcome even the steam and warmth. I don't know, would it?'

'It must have done, for whoever it was', Chris says practically. 'But you're like me, you haven't been upset either. That's a good point, Mum. Has anyone seemed upset, post murdering someone?'

We ponder. We can't think of anyone.

'Let's go on with the list', says Chris. 'Ron isn't there, is he?'

'No, he went off a while ago.'

'He's a bit odd, and lonely, and we don't know much about him. He sleeps in a coffin. That's pretty weird. Perhaps he knew Henry before and there's something in the past we don't know about, some huge motive.'

'Could be, Chris. Poor man. He's a possible, but ...'

We look at each other. It's always 'but ...' It's so hard to imagine anyone you've met as a murderer.

'Andy?'

'Andy!!! The cleanest-cut, least sleazy person in the whole camp! The least likely of anyone! Surely not!'

'Andy and Ron were both on the scene', recalls Chris.

'Well, I suppose so. Put them down as possible. Goodness knows what has happened in their pasts, what Henry might have done to them.'

'Then there's everyone else, the fathers and brothers and boyfriends of women Henry sleazed on.'

'It doesn't seem enough, though, does it?'

'We might have to assume that for one person, there's something else, something terrible enough to be a real motive', I muse.

'I suppose there is the question of who'd know how to strangle anyone', said Chris. 'But it's the same, the unknown quantity, who's done some course or other.'

'Not the sort of thing they teach in Adult Education', I say. 'Or in classes here, for that matter. Anarchy — Fire Twirling — Strangulation. Not very likely.'

'I think they teach it in armies', says Chris. 'The tougher ones.'

'Russians. I bet they're good at strangling. Chinese, Israelis. They're all what you might call pro-active armies', I muse. 'Probably even the commando-type bits of other armies. But no one seems very military here.'

'No', says Chris. 'They'd hate it. And HipHaven wouldn't take kindly to them.'

'Strangling someone wouldn't leave marks on the strangler, would it? I'm not too good on strangling. Agatha preferred little-known poisons, or stabbing. Probably because strangling seems to leave so few clues.'

'I wonder if the police have any more clues than we have', says Chris. 'I can't think how they could.'

'It's not like Agatha', I say. 'By now, Hercule would be saying it's like a jigsaw puzzle, and he has everything but the last tiny piece. And during the day some chance remark would give it to him. We haven't used our little grey cells enough, Chris. But really, there are no clues to use them on.'

There's a stirring from Andy's tent and with a shock I realise he can probably hear everything we're saying. He emerges, tousled, pale, unhappy. Poor boy.

'Come and have a cup of tea, Andy', I say. 'And how about — have we got anything to eat, Chris? Slim pickings by now', I explain to Andy.

Chris scrimmages round in the box and finds another packet of biscuits, the almond ones she bought for me. 'Just the thing', she says. 'They won't have gone off.'

'Oh, I can't take your food', says Andy, politely but unconvincingly.

'Andy, Chris doesn't like them and I can't possibly eat a whole packet of biscuits in one day', I say, 'It would be so bad for me! Save me from myself, do.' I pass over the packet. He smiles wanly, poor boy, and takes one. It vanishes pretty fast. Chris finds some grapes, still quite edible, only a little bit brown at the ends. They vanish too. So does a cup of tea. 'Do have another biscuit', I say. He does.

I wonder if he's homesick. Once a friend of Chris's we took away on holiday with us was terribly homesick. The only way to help, I found, was to encourage her to talk about her family. 'What do you suppose your family's doing right now, Andy?' I ask.

He looks surprised. 'I don't know', he says.

'What would they be having for breakfast?'

'Coffee?' he says. This doesn't seem to be very successful. What next?

'You know, I ...' he says, and stops. 'I ...'

'Spit it out, Andy', I say encouragingly.

'See if we can help', adds Chris.

He opens his mouth, shuts it, opens it again — and there's a cheerful call from Ron. 'Morning, all! Mind if I play my flute?'

'Lovely!' Chris and I chorus, of course. This is HipHaven. Andy is silent. He goes back into his tent. Jethro Tull fills the air. Great. Wonderful, of course it is, but it doesn't help Andy much.

'I don't think we're going to solve this mystery', I say to Chris. 'After all, Agatha Christie was writing fiction.'

'Remember that Famous Five you got for me?' she says. 'The one where someone said a parcel of children were better at solving mysteries than Scotland Yard? I think he was wrong.'

'For heaven's sake, when you write your autobiography don't put in that I gave you the Famous Five to read', I say. 'Didn't I give you anything more literate? I must have. Robin Klein.' We drift into discussing children's authors. Ron moves on to another composer whose name on the music book is too small for me to read and pretend to know just by the music.

'Mum', says Chris, 'we haven't done any body painting. Let's go.'

'Good!' I say. I've seen the body painting tent. It's always humming with activity, people painting and being painted and mixing up paints and finding they've sat on paints, and generally enjoying themselves.

We walk along the dusty paths — dust is very soft, lovely to walk on — and find a spare spot in the tent. Everyone's painting, from kids to grandparents. Chris strips off and I start on her back. What a canvas! So big and clean and empty, just waiting to be covered in wonderful swirls of colour. I paint a tree with wild waves of leaves, in green and yellow and orange and just a dab of blue in places. Then dots of white in empty spaces.

'Your go.' So I strip off and Chris has a go on my back. It's almost natural to be nude by now, from the waist up anyway — almost. Not quite. This is daylight. But she paints on, and the kids next door paint on, and it's all very relaxed. (But later I find it's hard to get the paint off my clothes.) Chris does some wonderful pattern that despite the mirror I can't really make out, but like me she has a great time doing it. Then we go back for a lazy lunch of leftovers.

Afterwards we sit idly watching as Nimrod practises his fire-twirling. No fire yet, but he has the stick, whatever it's really called, and he's very seriously doing the balancing and the turning and twisting, slowly getting the hang of it, like a faun weaving and bowing in time to internal music. I'd love to have a go, but don't like to interrupt. It's more arcadian rapture, this, with the sun's rays gleaming between the silver tree trunks, the beautifully moving little boy, and a flight of silver-crested cockatoos to add darting beauty. Their harsh squawks don't do much for the aural beauty, but doesn't every arcadia have its snake, or adder, or something? Or am I in the wrong haven? I'm half asleep, anyway.

Daughter

'Mum, it's the last day', says Chris. 'What will we do?'

'I don't know, darling.'

'I'm half inclined to go and visit my friends. They've been coming here for years, and they're up late and one of them might have seen something. If anyone has a theory, it will be them. Also, they're connected to the dodgier element.'

'That's fine, darling. If I get bored here I can always go to the craft tent.'

'OK, I'll go then and see what I can find out. Hercule wouldn't have given up now.'

After a quick hug, I head off down the track. It's a lovely afternoon, 28 degrees with a crisp breeze. My favourite weather. Some people have started packing up already and I see some highly organised activity — a well-packed truck that's been snuck in near the tents, somehow, with young men loading lounge chairs and a coffee table. Also, I see people squabbling about what goes where. I look away to give them some privacy.

The chanting tent is going strong. They've got a guitar out in the middle of a ring of people singing happily. Some of them look at me, like, 'Join us!' and I look away, as if I'm off to the loo.

The loos are still running OK, they're not full yet and there's only a short queue at this time of the day. I won't need to follow the timeless advice of Larry: 'If the loos start to stink, like really stink, go home because everyone is about to get sick.' I think the festival having crisply defined start and end times prevents large-scale food poisoning, but I could be wrong. I've always assumed Larry was right, and usually keep an eye, or a nose, on the state of the lavatories.

I have no idea where my mates are, so I head in the direction of their usual camp on the edge of the car park and start casting around. They camp up on the flat plain because they have a lot of heavy stuff. Mum and I travelled (with difficulty) to the lower, forested region beside the river, where cars are forbidden, but the buddies camp in the general trashbag area where you have cars and tents all in together, and the sun beating down on everything all day long. I stand in one spot and do a slow rotate, looking for their cars. Aha! I see Kylie's Delica and Sam's Delica. Danny's Combo. Little creatures of habit that they are.

You can't see much from the outside because everyone parks their car beside their tent. From the outside, it has the tenty, carparky feel of the rest of the festival. Hidden between the cars, though, is a large living space. I push aside a curtain made from a sarong and enter the camp of the buddies. Inside, it's surprisingly organised. It's entirely roofed in by tarps and there are strategic sarongs strung up as partial walls, ensuring there is a breeze but rarely a wind. Seven or eight tents surround the main living area. There are overlapping carpets on the floor, with tarps beneath them. There is very little dust here. In the central section is a ring of camp chairs, with beanbags and floor cushions. There are several low tables. On my right is a well-stocked kitchen area, with five eskies, a sink, a large water vat, two illegal stoves and an assortment of cooking implements.

On my left is a corral of drums, ready to be deployed in-tent or taken to tonight's drumming spot. There are buddies all over the place — sprawled on cushions, occupying chairs, in tents or just napping on the floor. There is also food everywhere, and beer. Nicole is across the room from me.

'Aah yeah! Ya came!'

'I got a leave pass from Mum. She's at the craft tent, making things.'

'Aay Chris,' says Huw, stretching up an arm.

'Hey bro,' I hold his hand, briefly.

'Oh, hi,' says Gordon, brightly packing a bong. He puts it down and steps forward for a hug.

''Ere she is,' Ray is next in line, crushing me in a man hug against his chest.

I feel great relief at being at the camp of the buddies. They understand me here. I can be my absolute self. If I'm tired, I can sleep. If I'm hungry, I can eat. This place is very easy.

We're a bit like water buffaloes on a nature documentary, our main occupations are grazing and socialising. It's here and in camps like this that I've had some of the best and most vulnerable conversations of my life. Because the pace is slow and you're not cut off by having to rush off somewhere, or check the train timetable, or needing to get things done. Our social connections are the things we need to get done, instead.

I plonk next to Nicole. Everyone returns to their conversations, bongs or naps.

'Hey, I can make a string water bottle holder.'

'Git fucked!'

'Nah, yeah, get me some string!'

'There's some builders' twine in the ute.' I go out to the ute, which is unlocked.

'Where in the ute?' I yodel over the tents.

'Not there. In the cab, on the floor with all the shit.'

'Yeah, got it. We need cushions. You got scissors?'

'Ciggie lighter.'

'What kind of stoner doesn't have scissors?'

'They're in the tent.'

'Stretch out your arms and hold out your thumbs. Twelve times your outstretched arms. There. Giz the lighter. We have to cut all of them. There ya go.'

'What do I do with these?'

'Hold on a sec, I'll just do mine ... OK. You tie a knot at the bottom.'

'Seriously,' I say. 'My mum and I've got some serious Miss Marple shit going. You need to help us find the killer of the Henry. After you've made me a cup of tea.'

'I was just gunna,' Nic says, putting her orange macramé down and heading toward the kitchen. I scout around for some cups to wash. Most of them have a smear of purple paint on the bottom, meaning they were originally burgled from the chai tent in the market. I find two and wash them in the sink and put them in front of Nicole. She's unscrewing a container of teabags. She sniffs a bag and frowns. Is it peppermint, or has it been stored with peppermint? I hug her, spontaneously. She's such a throwback to the Neanderthal era — so physical, always sniffing or tapping or breaking things.

'Yeah, this is just like Shibari,' Nic says, when we sit back down with our cups of tea and start knotting string again. 'We've been doing this Japanese rope bondage workshop in Melbourne when we can get down. You'd like it, you like knots.'

'You're making harnesses?'

'Nah, simple stuff. Little set of cuffs to put your hands behind your back, like this.' She puts her hands behind her back and looks at me cheekily over one shoulder. I might be into tying people up but really, it seems like a lot of fiddling around to have the sex you were going to have anyway.

Putu wanders over and starts fiddling with a tarp.

'Hey man, I saw a movie about Indonesia recently.'

'The love story?'

'No, it was about the massacres in '68.'

'Oh yes, I was five then. My dad was one of the people they went to kill. The communist massacres.'

'Oh, I thought they ...'

'They would accuse you of being a communist and kill you. They came to kill my dad. But his friend was high up and he said, "He is not political, he is just a mechanic." So they went away. It could have gone the other way. They would take you away, slice off your head.'

'They talked about that in the film. If they did that in Australia, us hippies would be the first ones to be murdered.'

'That's why I like it here. The people are educated. There, they are not so educated and they might kill you because of a rumour.'

'Heard a talk the other day, Indonesia has one of the largest education systems in the world, now.'

'It's getting better now, yeah.' And off he goes, probably to his van, which is the size of a suburb and has a full kitchen, bed and hammock in it.

Aww. It's the Russians, emerging from a nap. People call them the Dodgy Russians because they have a certain unorthodox way of getting things done, but I call them the Darling Russians, to focus on their many positive qualities.

Anton, or Doctor Anton, as we call him, is small and bouncy and is wearing a couple of days' stubble and a striped t-shirt. He's one of those health nuts you can approach with any ailment, and he'll have a solution. He can also access a range of substances that are more exotic than anyone else in the gang, with the possible exception of Gordon, though I wouldn't be keen to put it to the test.

The other Darling Russian is Michel. I'll admit, there is something about him. He comes out of a tent that is absolutely bare of all possessions. There are several lengths of rope by the door, stored exactly the way I like them — neatly coiled and tied. I've seen campers with bags of tangled rope, and they give me a queasy feeling in my stomach.

Michel is lithe and lean with blue-green eyes and sandy hair, and practises some extreme form of martial art. He has the strength of several of us puny alternative types. At the moment, he looks as if he's only here under sufferance, and if anyone said, 'Let's go and build a tree platform in the forest,' he'd be gone. Or if anyone said, 'We attack at dawn,' he'd be putting on camo paint and sharpening his combat knife within a minute.

You know how some military people never quite lose that look? He's never quite lost that look. Anton and Michel were born in a communist country, and retain an entrenched sense of dubiousness about the democratic process. Their facebook accounts bear no mention of their real names, and I've heard them claim that 'Governments are just gangs,' on several occasions.

Cass strolls up, waves and sits on a chair. A profound and lifelong conspiracy theorist, she is red hot where the Russians are cold. 'The collapse may be coming,' she says. I'd be disappointed if she didn't. 'I've heard from Nui. The banks are wobbling, exactly as predicted. It's definitely time to withdraw some cash and maintain supplies if you're into prepping. Nui's mortgage is due at the end of the month, and they wanted the money at the start of the month. They've never wanted it then before. They're desperate for cash. Absolutely desperate. So where did the cash go?'

Oh no, she's looking straight at me. Was I even paying attention? Where *did* the cash go? Am I supposed to know? I shrug.

'Exactly. There's a plughole in global finance and all the cash is going in there, but whose plughole is it? Whose plughole is it.' She sits in a fug of bitter rumination.

Kaela blithers over, off her tits on psychedelics. She sits conspicuously on a fallen mattress and her blonde hair falls over her eyes. She looks at Nicole, who has abandoned her string water bottle holder and is packing a bong.

'You shouldn't be bonging on,' says Kaela. 'You were doing so well. Oh, I seem not to have a filter right now.'

'Well, mushies'll do that,' I say, placatingly.

'Oh yeah, there were the mushies. I mean ...'

'Well, you haven't got a filter at the best of times,' says Nic.

Kalea winds up and lets fly. 'You know what? You can be a real bitch. You're just nasty. You say all these horrible things all the time. I'm sick of it. You always do it, you've done it to heaps of people. I don't think you even think.'

'It's just the way I am, darl. I'm not gunna change.'

'Well, you should.'

There's a bit of a huffy silence.

The Russians have a bag of what looks like twigs and they're passing them round the group and people are eating them. Everyone looks a bit like a pod of gorillas, sitting around eating twigs. No doubt the twigs are some dubious import with a mild narcotic effect.

'What are they?' I ask, waving at the bag.

'We got them in from Kenya,' says Anton.

'Oh.'

'They are a mild narcotic. Go on and have some!'

I give the twigs a miss, and they circulate on their own. If anyone killed Henry, I don't think it was my mates because they are the first camp I've been to since the murder that looks completely relaxed. Apart from Cass, no one is fretting about it even slightly.

'So, how 'bout the dude in the steam tent?' asks Gordon. 'Murdered.'

OK, maybe I was wrong.

'Weird, uh?' I say.

'Who do ya think did it?'

'Maybe he sleazed onto the wrong woman for once,' I say. 'Not to speak ill of the dead, of course.'

'That guy was so sleazy,' says Huw. 'He was feral. He came onto Cat one time when she was seven months pregnant.'

'Yeah,' says Cat. 'He asked if he could rub my belly and then he kept going down.'

'That old trick, eh?' says Nicole. 'That one's so old, it takes its teeth out before it goes to bed at night.'

'It flew spitfires in the War,' I add.

At that point, everyone starts in on the sleazy Henry stories. There sure are a lot of them. But no-one seems to know anything about Henry besides his sexual vileness. He lives in the twilight zone of the seasoned overtalker. He talks so much, people are sort of repelled, and no one ever gets close enough to find out anything about him.

Then Cass chimes in. I don't know how, but she has actual facts about him. 'He used to be part-owner of a farm, out near Bendigo,' she says. 'I think he had sheep there. Maybe five years ago.'

I remember seeing him in a town out that way, when I was visiting. 'Who did he own the farm with?' I ask.

'Some guy. They were making pickles, I think. The guy was European. Their business was going well, but they fell out because Henry and the other guy's wife started a thing.'

'Oh.'

'The other guy was upset and he left Henry with nothing. Then the woman left as well. Henry's been touring ever since.' Sometimes festival people go touring for a year or two, taking a van and going from festival to festival and staying in people's farms and driveways.

'He didn't have a house?'

'Don't think so.'

The Darling Russians have been brewing tea. They get a tiny glass pot and any number of tea packets from a little suitcase. There are also some small cups without handles.

'Would you like some tea?' asks Dr Anton.

'What is it?'

'Silver needle tea. It's from China. They drink it to celebrate weddings. It tastes like butterscotch.'

'Yes please.' Dr Anton hands me a little cup of pale, hot tea. It does taste like butterscotch.

'It's lovely.'

'Yes. I am sorry. We normally have a second large cup to mix the tea in. It evens out the flavour between the first and second cups. So yours is a little weak, and mine is a little strong.'

'Oh, it's great. Really.'

'No, no. We will bring the large cup next time.'

'So, how's your festival been?'

'Good. We ignored the river ban, and we got a little itchy. So we swam again in the moonlight, and that was a little bit better. Also Michel's van broke down and it took nine hours to arrive here. But we have had a good time mostly relaxing and playing drums.'

'I'm over this drink bottle holder.' Nicole chimes in.

'Oh, you're nearly there! That's a shame!'

'Yeah, but me back's sore.'

'Don't do it if it hurts your back.'

'I'm leaning forward too much.'

'Well, can you sit somewhere else?'

'Yep, here we go.'

'You're only two rows away. Then it's plaiting. You've done gymkhana, you can plait.'

'I can't do it neat like you're doing.'

'Mate, it's a water bottle holder. No one cares. Just tie it off.'

'The fuck am I bothering?'

'Sure, you'll have some butterscotch tea, won't you?'

Dr Anton's mate Michel, having had tea, is stretched out lengthwise on a mattress in the sun. It's an impressive sight. He's a grim, muscly sort of a dude. I always want to give him a cupcake or something. He looks as if there's been a fundamental lack of sweetness in his life. He stretches, opens his eyes a crack.

'Who killed Henry, Michel?'

'I do not care,' he says fiercely, swatting with his hand. 'These guys, they come up to the festival, kill a hippie who never harmed anyone. I have no time for that. I have not one second for that person.'

'Yeah. Why would anyone want that guy dead?' asks Anton. 'He was annoying, it's true. But many people are annoying. They don't ever get killed. It's not that for sure. Someone had an actual reason to want him dead. A proper motive, I believe. Someone held a grudge against him.'

Michel springs up in a single, catlike motion. I stand by the mild crush I have on him. I have excellent judgement.

'Anton is right,' he says. 'If you are going to strangle someone, as he was strangled, you must hold their windpipe closed for at least a minute. And he would be struggling the whole time. And he is a big man. Old, but still strong. He would be hitting you. Look for someone with bruises.' He demonstrates the physics of his assertions by mock-strangling Dr Anton, who throws out some fake blows. It's obvious that it would take strength and determination to kill anyone that way.

'So it was someone who really hated Henry,' I say.

'It was not a small emotion,' says Michel. 'Not irritation, not pettiness, not spite. It was not the guy whose wife was taken, because he had already made him pay. It was someone else.' And he lies down in the sun again and closes his eyes.

'You all need to stop worrying about it,' says Vic. 'It's like when Anand died. You all worried yourselves sick over it for years and forgot to enjoy what you had. Henry's dead now. He's gone, he's fully gone. There isn't anything you can do about that, ever. You're not going to bring him back. You're not going to heal his spirit or whatever. Someone was seriously pissed off. You can't fix them, either. They're probably still seriously pissed off. You can't probably help them, coz they're not gonna talk about it. So stop worrying about it and enjoy.' He waves an arm at the camp setting. 'Enjoy,' he says, a little hopelessly. This was quite a long speech for Vic, and everyone is silent for a good minute out of respect for the effort he has extended.

'Well, it couldn't have been a family member,' says Gordon. Vic growls, sighs and walks off.

'Why not?' asks Nic.

'He doesn't have any.'

'Doesn't he?' I ask. Everyone has someone.

'Like, who would put up with a dork like him in their family?'

'Have you *seen* most families?'

'Hey Chris, why didn't your mum come?' Asks Nic.

'I wasn't a million percent sure I could find you guys, and I didn't want to drag her over here for nothing,' I say. 'Also, there's stuff on at the craft tent.'

'She's not avoiding us?'

'Mate, she doesn't know you! But get real, you have tea and good food, she'd love you if she was here. But it's her first festival like this one and I didn't want to overwhelm her with people.'

I sense that I'm not going to get much more useful info out of the buddies, and I'm starting to worry about Mum, even though she's a highly resilient adult person, and is probably making tea.

'I gotta go check in on Mum,' I say to the group.

'Are ya going, ya cahn?' says Nicole. 'Fine then, piss off.'

She stretches out her arms from the banana lounge, refusing to budge. I lean over and hug her.

'See ya, guys,' I say. I hug Cass as well, and Anton.

'Watch where the money goes,' says Cass, fiercely, in my ear. 'The money tells the story.'

Mother

What will I do now? Something interesting. Another workshop? Yes, that's it, something I'd never dream of doing at home. I walk to the board with all the amazing subjects people are giving workshops about. Really, people are constantly surprising. Vibrational geometric medicine. Lucid dreaming and astral travelling. Transforming cellular memory. Whoever would be able to talk for an hour about that — and whoever would want to listen? Be fair, Sally. Who wants to read the history of a credit union, the one I wrote a few years ago.

What do I know nothing about? Well, that's easy, a lot of them. I read on. Aha, here's the one: Equinox vision quest: Remake your life. It's on in ten minutes, so I go. Next to the river, near the Arts Beach.

I'm confident now, at HipHaven. I can find my way. Our workshop is beside another one that's for something called 'nude laughter'. People are sitting naked in a big, loose circle, and a woman with long grey-brown hair is standing in the middle, giving instructions. There are a few stragglers at the back, peeling off socks and shedding ponchos.

I join the dozen or so others who want to remake themselves, and we sit on the cushions on friendly old deep-red patterned rugs — 'old' in the sense of 'made forty years ago', not 'antique', so you don't mind lolling around on them with your dirty feet. I'm beside charming Vivienne of the Craft Café, the one who reminded me of a benign high priestess. I tell her so and she laughs. She's still wearing floaty indigo and silver garments and I can't imagine why she wants to remake herself. She looks perfect as she is. Next door, the people start chuckling and giggling. It's quite distracting, especially when they all slap their tummies and shout with laughter.

The workshop-runner arrives. She's short, thin, cheerful, bouncing with energy and friendliness. 'Hi!' she beams. 'I'm Roxy Rocky-Rock. That's my Skype name, but you can call me Rocky-Rock. Or you can call me Elphie. Elphie with a ph.' I don't think my mouth could form the words 'Rocky-rock' as a name for anyone, so I settle for Elphie. Though Elfie suits her better, since she had an elfin look. Ephie sounds too elephantine. Enough! Sternly, I bring my mind back to the workshop topic.

Elphie explains that this workshop-cum-experience-cum-life-rebuilding exercise is usually done at an equinox or solstice. We'll be doing a concentrated version. In the real thing, you start three days before the equinox. On the first day you meditate on what you want to bless and release from your life. You write down everything you think of during the twenty-four-hour period. On the second day you ask what you want to maintain in your life. And on the third, what you want to bring into your life. On the equinox itself, there's a big ceremony around a fire and you burn the paper. Then you have the most wonderful, incredible feeling of liberation. 'I was blown away by the lightness of being I felt after that process', says Elphie. 'All the baggage being released.' I remember feeling the same after the one time I made my confession, even though I only made it in the hopes of being made a prefect at school. I imagine God up in heaven rolling her eyes and groaning, 'Another hypocrite'.

I'm torn away from these unworthy thoughts by Elphie giving out paper (unlined, so we have no outside guidance) and pencils. Instead of a day we have only fifteen minutes per section.

'It is feelings we want to get rid of, or people, or what?' I ask her.

'Everything!' she exclaims, her face lighting up. 'Everything you want to lose!'

'Why do we bless them first?' asks a thin, intense young man.

'We bless them for the lessons they've taught us', says Elphie, 'Everything has its shadow side.'

'My stepfather?' says someone else. Elphie nods: anyone, anything. People scribble away. Bad temper. Impatience, intolerance, I write, though a few days at HipHaven has increased my tolerance and ebbed away impatience. I can't think of any people to write down. Appetite, I put. Bad habit of interrupting people. They're getting noisier next door, and I feel like adding, 'nude laughter workshops'. It would be too mean to add 'bicycle bells' and 'small irritating children'. I suppose I bless all these things as Elphie requested, but more in the mood of saying 'You blessed pest!' than actual blessings. Why is there suddenly such a lot of blessing in the world? People are always saying they're blessed with something or other, even if they never go near a place of worship. No one used to. Stop it, Sally, I chide, there's nothing wrong with it. It's you that's at fault for being critical, not people for saying perfectly admissible things, like 'incredible' about things that are perfectly believable, and 'so' used as the wrong part of speech — is it an adverb? I include 'grammatical intolerance' in my list.

I sneak a look at Vivienne's list. It's very long. I'm puzzled. How could she have major faults, and who or what could she possibly dislike enough to put on her list? A disease, perhaps? I scribble 'arthritis'. It doesn't seem likely that burning its name will make it vanish, but disbelief will not help here. Perhaps believing it will go helps reduce the pain. A more interesting placebo than a pill.

We move on to the next section. What do we want to maintain in our lives? This is easy. Practically everything. All the people — bar a few I wouldn't mind not seeing again

— my house, my family, my activities and particularly my friends. I quite like me as I am, were I a bit more tolerant, patient etc. I like my work, writing history. In fact I'm even missing it, a bit. I'm glad to see Vivienne's list is nice and long. They'd certainly have long lists at the nude laughter workshop. The level of hilarity is sky-high. How can they keep it up? Dirty limericks? Funny stories? That grey-haired leader has great gusto and stamina, that's for sure. She snortles through a sentence and they all bellow anew with uproarious laughter. Perhaps I'm just envious.

'Now remember,' says Elfie. 'We're not human beings on a spiritual journey, we're spiritual beings on a human journey. We're now writing down all the things we want to introduce into our lives. Remembering that everything has an opposite — day and night, happy and sad. Sometimes when we want to bring in more of something, we must be prepared to embrace the shadow side as well. The equinox is about balance.'

Oh, for heaven's sake, I think. I don't believe everything does have an opposite. What about trees? What's the opposite of a tree? Or a flower? But it doesn't seem kind to upset the atmosphere of happy naivete that HipHaven has created. Though who's been naïve about drugs?

Anyway, I have to think of some things I want to introduce into my life. The people next door link arms in a big circle and lean back chuckling and bellowing. One of them barks like a dog, and then they all do. Someone makes oinking noises, and they echo around the circle. At an instruction from their leader they all collapse on to all fours and start snuffling round on the floor of the tent. I can't bear to watch. I look away, trying not to seem snippy.

Quick, what do I want to introduce? Peace. Into my perfectly peaceful life — well it would be if I didn't have to look at people's bums, like that strange ululating woman, and *must* they all bend over like that? I look away again. Prude, I tell myself.

Happiness. Happiness for everyone. It seems crass to say money. I can't think. God, they're not being dogs copulating next door, are they? No, thank heavens, just dogs being playful. Oh no, not lifting their legs! They move into a deep belly-laughing section, going 'ho ho ho,' in unison like so many naked Father Christmases.

Oh dear, must write something. Success in writing. Happy children. Good health. That'll do.

Elphie calls us to order. 'All finished?' I wonder if we have to hand our bits of paper in for marking. I might not pass. But no, we all file over to a nearby fire circle, where Elphie has some twigs laid out in half a large drum. She lights them, and one by one we consign our dreams and wishes to the flames. Some people say a few words. 'Off you go,' I say, and then remember I wrote down the things I wanted as well.

Vivienne watches the smoke from her list with a look of sadness. The intense man comments about how hard it was not to write down 'money'. Someone else makes a mock salute to his list as he burns it. Several people hold their lists as they burn, and there are squeals as the flames nip their fingers.

But in the end they're all burnt. 'Would anybody like to share any thoughts?' asks Elphie. 'Safe space — you don't need to share anything you don't want to.' There is a pause. 'You don't need to be anything you don't want to. Just be here among the loveliness.'

'Thanks, Elphie, that was wonderful', says Vivienne.

'Very cathartic', adds Mr Intense.

'I enjoyed it', I said truthfully, though it would have been better in a quieter setting. But that's my fault, for not being able to concentrate better. It's nothing to do with Elphie. She's been good, so enthusiastic and encouraging.

'Boy, I needed to get all that drawing out about my Dad', says the saluting man. 'I didn't even *know* it was — well, I knew a *bit* of it was — but I didn't know it was all in there. I thought it was my mother!'

'You can actually do this process at any time,' says Elphie. 'It's just that equinox and solstice are particularly significant times to do it.'

The nude laughter people are being cleared out for the next workshop. Some stride off, proudly naked, while others reclothe, becoming more normal — more boring? — with every garment.

'Do you feel the lightness of being Elphie was talking about?' I ask the people near me.

'Yes, I do feel lighter,' says Vivienne. 'Wonderfully lighter.'

'That sort of spiritual claptrap always makes me feel lighter', comments the saluting man, picking up his multi-coloured felted manbag and departing. This is a bit hard on Elphie, I feel, and give her the biggest smile I can.

'That workshop next door was a bit irrit—, er, distracting, wasn't it?' I remark to Vivienne as we walk off.

'Was it?' she says. 'I didn't notice.'

Daughter

I'm coming back when I bump into my old friend Narah. She is the oldest friend I have here — we used to party together back in my university days.

'Oh wow, I didn't know you were going to be here!' I say, giving her a hug.

'Oh hey Chris, yeah, I've been going to festivals all over Australia, you gotta get out to the Central Desert, they run a ceremony like you wouldn't believe, there are so many massive festivals and parties and they just come together on the full moon, the dark moon, and they happen all the time. I was out there with Nadia —'

I don't know who Nadia is.

'— and she said to me, girl, check this sunset. And the sunsets out there, they are this lovely, warm, really golden colour —'

I've lived near the central desert. I know the sunsets.

'— and they light up the whole sky. They can go on for hours, depending on the time of year. They're really special. These sunsets here are pretty good. I like the clouds in this part of the world. Particularly last night, did you see them? There was an altostratus overlying a horsetail cirrus. It's one of my favourite combinations. So many people don't look up. They just don't look up, they look down and they get depressed and then they get on antidepressants like that's a normal thing to do. I want to say to them "Look up! Look up and live your life!" This culture is so fucking stupid. And Nadia says, I dunno if we're really smart or really lucky. Look at where we are in the world —'

She's still talking about the Central Desert. But right now we're in a pretty special part of the world, too.

'— and I'm like yeah, we're smart all right. Think of all the people in the cities, they're in offices, and they're going to the gym. I hate the gym.'

I go to the gym. It helps with the arthritis.

'It's full of people in lycra, like you can exercise in a building with fifty other people all round you. If you want to get fit, you get a manual job. I was fruitpicking for years, and during that time I never needed any exercise, ever. All those people are in the gym and we're out here in the clean air, watching this magical sunset with our friends, and all the things we need are right here. Fred took me out the other week —'

I don't know who Fred is.

'— and he wasn't even noticing the sunset, I said, "Fred, I want you to look up, right now". Seriously, there were mamma clouds and virga right on the horizon, this amazing combination, virga is rain that doesn't reach the ground —'

I used to sail with international pilots. I know what virga are.

'— and mamma are the clouds that hang down like breasts, they're named mamma after breasts —'

118

I know about mamma. I know the derivation of their name.

'— and Fred was taking me out to the Provencale for dinner because it was the anniversary of his divorce from his second wife. He calls it our Second Chanciversary. He takes me out every year because he says if he didn't get the second chance of his wife leaving him, he'd never have met me when we all went camping. It's hard work, relationships are always difficult —'

Technically, she's his third chance.

'— and Fred sometimes struggles with depression, and anxiety. It's like being stuck under a table. The depression pulls you down, and then the anxiety gets you up, only you bang your head on the table and fall back down again. It's a trap. Fred struggles a lot. I think he needs to eat more fish but he won't because we're more than a hundred k from the ocean —'

Still no idea who Fred is, but from the context I am gathering that he is her long-term partner.

'— but they snap freeze it on the docks. He says he won't eat it because what if the truck broke down on the way to the market. Also he goes fishing himself so to him, fish are free and it's weird to pay for them. Personally, I think all food should be free. It's weird to pay for food full stop —'

I am looking down and looking away and trying vainly to get out of this conversation. I've remembered how terribly tedious these long and seamless monologues are from the last time we were friends. I've remembered why we don't catch up now and then. I've remembered that inner screaming I do when I am being held in a conversation against my will. I've remembered how incredibly sensitive she is and how hurt she will be if I make excuses and leave. Her life must be full of people making excuses and leaving.

'— because in the old days the food came from the commons and before that in the neolithic we were communally farming together and you wouldn't let a person in your tribe go hungry. That was in the time when there were no walls around the cities so they recognised that the people had no need for war —'

We don't have city walls now, and we've just come through the most violent century ever.

'— and they worshipped a goddess rather than a god. Women are more likely to look after the vulnerable in the community, they had a program in refugee camps in South East Asia where they stopped distributing the food on a grid, with a certain amount of food per square, that was the old way, and instead they delivered it to the women of the community, who ensured that everyone in the community got fed equitably —'

I am really looking around for a way out now.

'— and they measured the weight of the children and it went up because under the old way the food just went to the gang leaders and standover men, so the men got fed the most and the children got the least. Children were dying of malnutrition and of course, iodine deficiency —'

'Narah, my Mum's here.'

'Oh! You brought your mum! Coz I've got my friend Gerold who is seventy-eight —'

'And I've got to go and check on her. Good night!'

'If you're looking out for who killed Henry, you're probably looking in the wrong place. He was a rude person and he never considered the feelings of others, but nobody will kill him because of that. What you're looking for is a secret relationship like a lover or a family member. Have you asked if he's got family here? This was a crime with a lot of feeling in it. Nobody whose wife he screwed. Somebody with a real claim against him. Find that and you've got your murderer.'

'See ya later!' I am so keen to get away from the onslaught of half-baked ideas and teflon-coated social thought bubbles that I am halfway home before I realise she's said some things that might be really useful. It takes a rude person to know a rude person, and apart from Henry,

Narah is the rudest person I know. She might have insight that other people don't have. I'll run it past Mum.

I see Sarah coming along the track. I'm trying to hold in all the irritation and resentment I'm feeling about Narah, but unfortunately I can't help but bail Sarah up, even though she is a nice, quiet person. She is pale and slender and wearing a whimsical crocheted top and looking down and hunching in a little. 'Sarah, can I ask you something?'

'Yes,' she says in her musical voice.

'You're really quiet, right?'

'I guess so.'

'How do you stand it? I mean, doesn't everyone seem really rude and loud all the time?'

'I do spend a lot of time on my own because I like the peace. But I don't dislike everyone.'

'You don't feel like strangling them?'

'I mean, sometimes. You always feel like strangling some people, sometimes.'

'Thanks so much.'

'You're very welcome.'

'Was that a weird thing to ask?'

'Not at all. There are louder people and softer people. We're all important in our own way.'

She's the nicest person in the world. I realise I just used strangulation as my example, and the bottom drops out of my stomach for a moment.

Mum is in her chair, looking hungry.

'I'm sorry, Mum!' I say. 'People kept wanting to talk. Only sometimes it was me.'

'Did they say anything useful?' she asks.

'Well,' I say, getting out the chopping board and the olives.

'And then she talked and talked!' I say, handing Mum her dinner.

'I remember Narah,' says Mum. 'She told me that people with Ph.Ds are up themselves.'

'Oh Mum,' I say. 'I'm sorry she said that to you.'

'It's all right,' says Mum. 'I think she wants to show she's a little bit better than everyone she meets.'

'Yup,' I say. 'She just told me so for twenty minutes.'

'Does she have a job?' asks Mum.

'No.'

'Has she ever done anything?'

'Yes, she was a senior sales manager twenty years ago. I see where you're heading. The people I know who've done stuff, who've done amazing things, they're humble.'

Mum smiles at me. 'They are.'

'And the people who never do anything are the ones who talk a lot.'

'The less they do, the more they talk.'

'Mum,' I say. 'I talk a lot. And I haven't done anything.'

'Oh darling,' Mum says, reaching over and squeezing my hand. 'There's a bit of it in all of us. Remember Grandpa's stories?'

'He had so many stories.'

'Don't worry about Narah,' says Mum. 'She certainly isn't worrying about you.'

'The buddies who've done military training seem to think it's a major thing with Henry,' I say, switching tacks.

'I think we knew that.'

'Not just someone who he drove crazy. Someone close to him.'

'Hey guys,' says Andy.

'Hello there!' says Mum. 'We've got some salad we can't finish. There's a bowl on the stump.' The urge to serve young men vegetables is strong in the females of my family.

'I couldn't at all,' he says. 'You have it.'

'Very well. Biscuit?'

'No thank you.'

'Oh. Well, it looks like we can't feed you.'

'Do you mind if I tell you something?'

'Go ahead.'

'Henry had family here.'

'Oh, did he? Who?'

'I've been in my tent for two days, listening to you try to work it out. You're getting close.'

'Do you know who did it?' Mum seems to be taking all this in stride. My stomach is like a tennis ball, hard and round. If he knew already, why didn't he come forward? Why let a murderer walk round? It must have been one of his friends, he must have been covering for ...

'It was me.'

Mum really does drop her fork. I didn't know people actually did that. I'm in a sudden flash of fear. Mum's closest to him, he's behind her chair. I try not to let my eyes dart to where our sharp knives are sitting, next to the washing up tub.

I pick up Mum's fork and give it back to her, wiping it on my shorts. Normal! Let's do normal.

'What happened?'

'You know how I told you about my stepdad?'

'Yes.' Where is this going? Is he about to kill us both, now that we know?

'Henry's my —', he falters, and stops.

'Henry's your birth father.' Mum's always been more astute than me. I rub my thighs, which are clenched and won't seem to undo. I can smell a fear stink in the sweat that just broke out in my armpits. Andy's a murderer. Andy is Henry's murderer. Andy is a father-murderer. Does that make him a patricidal maniac? Shut up, brain. Focus.

I wrench my mind back to their conversation.

Mother

So, a lovely young man has just told me he murdered his father. I'm totally taken aback. I can only gape. What does a helpful, law-abiding person do now?

I pull myself together. He's a young man needing help, murderer or not. (The thought creeps into my mind, only of Henry, and is quickly suppressed.)

'Andy', I say. 'How terrible for you. I suppose he was awful to you, was he?'

'He was terrible to me, but he was worse to Mom. Violent. Horrible. I thought he was going to kill her. That's why we left him. He went back to Australia and I haven't heard of him for years. But now, at the festival, I realised who he was.'

'Andy', I say again. What else can I do? 'You didn't realise till you got here?'

'No. He's easily recognised. Just the same as he was then. And I remembered everything he'd done to Mom, and — I don't know, something happened, I can't remember really — and I found myself strangling him. And he went floppy and died.' He gulps, chokes, looks around helplessly.

I can't help it. 'How did you know how to?'

He looks a bit surprised, but answers readily enough. 'The army. The Israeli army. We moved to California, but I went back to do my training, to defend Israel.'

'What are you going to do now?'

'I don't know.' He says it pathetically. He obviously really doesn't know. Poor boy, I think — but he killed a man.

'Andy', says Chris gently, 'can you live with this knowledge for the rest of your life? If you can't, you'd be best to give yourself up.'

He looks horrified and bewildered. 'I have to go', he says, and wanders off disconnectedly. I wonder if he'll bump into a tree. Chris and I look at each other.

'We should have known, I suppose', she says. 'We were looking for someone who was upset, and who was the only person who was upset? Andy.'

'Remember the way he suddenly disappeared when Henry walked along the path? You know the time he took our photo? I thought it was a bit odd, at the time.'

'Yes, and the Israeli bit. We weren't very quick on the uptake, were we.'

'And who was it who said he was the least likely person? Me', I say. 'I was right in giving myself the halfwit sidekick role.'

Daughter

I'm wearing a poncho to ward off the chill of the night. The weird thing about drum circle, I think as I round the first aid tent and walk through the dust towards the market, is that it's never in the same place. Some nights it's pumping in the middle of the market, tacky and easily found by everyone, surrounded by lights and stalls and food. Other nights, it's by the river on sacred ground. Drums are always findable because they are loud instruments, but somehow they can become hidden and it's the older, seasoned crew that clusters round. And sometimes they're somewhere else altogether. What happens is as the mood strikes them, little crews of drummers head off to various venues and start to play. After that, it's a free market economy — if no-one comes, they pack up and go home. However, if people cluster around and start dancing, more drummers come and start playing, which calls in more dancers in a positive feedback loop and the whole thing cooks on until dawn.

The drummers aren't in the market, so I head around the back, where the generators and vans live. Beside a brightly lit van full of hanging beads, scarves and green ornaments stands an older guy. He's wearing a beanie and jacket and he has a week's worth of beard and crooked teeth. I recognise him from various camping ventures in the past. 'Wouldja like a cosmic hot chocolate?' he asks.

'Oh! Wow, what's in it?'

'Erm, raw cacao, evaporated cane juice, soy milk, cinnamon, mushies and MDMA,' he says.

'I'll pass,' I say. 'But thank you for your generosity.'

'No problems, my sister,' he says. 'We also have chips and dip.'

I stand for a while with him, eating his snacks. You never realise how hungry you are until you eat your first corn chip. My friend Alex wanders over. He's an addict in recovery. Even when he isn't looking for them, he managed to find the guy who's giving out drugs. Perhaps his addictive spirit drew him here.

'Mate,' I say when the owner of the van has gone inside, 'If anyone offers you something called a cosmic hot chocolate, the correct answer is no.'

'Oh wow! Thanks!' He says. 'I totally would have said yes, it sounds delicious!' And he bounces off, chip in hand, to enjoy his evening.

Eventually, I'm drawn further back. A warm scene awaits me, all the buddies are drumming around a fire, and the rhythm washes over me. Everyone has a golden side and a dark side; their faces are lit up by the fire and their backs are in the night. A wall of silhouettes stands in front of me. I weave through the crowd; a man in the throes of ecstasy leaning backwards and dancing, two young women in jeans and legwarmers flashing their eyes through the crowd. Nicole sees me and points to the empty drum beside her with her head. I leave my poncho at the rhythm drums and join her. There's a little three-legged drumming stool behind the spare drum. I sit down, tilt the drum slightly and grasp it with my knees. It's a nice drum, goatskin with red rope lacing. I tap experimentally. Nicole takes charge as she does, and leans back and plays a phrase on her drum, looking pointedly at me. I play the rhythm back at her. It's not perfect but she nods, and goes back to her playing.

I start playing my rhythm, which is tricky and not one I would ever have thought of. West African-style rhythms are all about the on-beat, not the beat, not the syncopated off-beat, but the gap between when you see the spider and when you scream. The microgap before the beat. Sometimes I get it, sometimes I don't. Eventually I figure out that I can breathe and play at the same time. The knuckles of my palm start to hurt. But I am making this drum ring. I think the wonderful thing about drumming is giving yourself permission to make a big loud noise, even if you're quiet, even if you're shy. We make this noise together.

I carefully don't look at the dancers because I'll forget where my hands are. Breathing in and out. Trying not to breathe with the rhythm in forced, shortened breaths. Breathing at the rhythm of my body. Sitting shoulder to shoulder with Nicole. Getting the rhythm right more often than I don't. Missing a beat now and then. Living by Gordon's mantra: 'Don't ruin the rest of the song worrying about one beat you missed at the start.' Gradually hearing more and more: the rhythm drums behind me. Gordon peacocking away to my left. The colours, all the black and gold around us. The freedom of the sky above. So much of life is lived in rooms, going from one to another. Now the sky is above us and we are free. Never under a ceiling, nor hemmed in by walls. The smiles of my friends across the fire. Red and gold and spitting and sparking.

If only Mum were here. I mean, I know she can't be. If she fell in the darkness it would be a catastrophe. But I wish she was here.

Mother

And now I finish my last Agatha Christie. It was all so straightforward for her. A horrible person is murdered — well, that's pretty well the story here — and Hercule or Miss Marple works out who has done it, from a long list of suspects. There are interesting clues and it's a clever piece of deduction with satisfying result, a person you didn't think of as the murderer but don't really care about, not the hero or heroine or anyone nice. And this person gets arrested, or dies accidentally, or something. Here, Chris and I didn't deduce anything, and Andy told us the result, and now what do we do? I hate this. I toss and turn and throw myself around the chair, then go to bed and toss and turn there.

OK, I tell myself, let's be logical here. What are my options?

One. Tell the police. This is the correct behaviour for a law-abiding citizen. A murderer has confessed his crime. The police should be told. But I can't do it. He's an unhappy young man, it's not as if there's anyone else he feels the same way about, it's not as if Henry's any great — no, no, that's unfair and not legal. But still. I can't do it. So that leaves me with Option Two: silence.

TUESDAY

Daughter

I'm sweaty. We try to love the packup, my friends and I. Gordon always heartily says, 'I love the packup. I love getting all kinds of horrible, greasy things that have gone everywhere and gotten covered in dirt and bark and sunscreen, and putting them in little piles. I love sorting out what to do with the food that's gone off. I love putting dirty socks into bags.' Those are hollow, hollow words.

Anyway, it's hot in a sort of vestigial way, and I'm lumping my bloody annoying massive throne chair to the car. Sweat is starting to prickle and the chair bumps against my shins and I'm worried Mum will do things and hurt herself. My shorts are baggy and threatening to fall down. Fucking packing. Thank Jesus I was able to park in closer. Of course, I didn't come and park in closer for an hour and pack the stuff and move the car back out to the baking campsite in the middle of nowhere. That would have been foolish. No, once the car was in, it stayed in until all the sleeping was done and the meals were eaten, so we could pack up and get ready to go.

This trip didn't go at all according to plan. I mean, there wasn't a plan. But if there had been one, then this trip wouldn't have adhered to it at all. There was a murder. There were cops in a van. Other, normal stuff also happened, like dancing and drumming and painting each other's backs with non-toxic body paint. But this murder business was weird. And we know who the murderer is, and no-one else does. Not the cops, not the organisers, not the one person, somewhere, who genuinely cared for Henry and was sad to see him go. And we know that he was the birth father to a very lovely, if fatally unbalanced young man. I haven't even seen Andy this morning. His grasshopper green tent has not moved at all. I think he might be lying low until we leave. I would be, if I were in his position. I hope his bladder isn't bursting, that he's got a spare bottle or something in there. Mum and I will be at least another hour packing up our stuff.

At the car, I plonk the chair down on the ground while I wrestle with the door of the boot. Dammit, I got this fixed and now it's broken again. I wearily walk to the driver's side door and lock and unlock the car a few times. It sorts it out, but it's time to take the car to the mechanic again. Why am I thinking about this when there's a murderer in a tent, about to totally get away with it?

Mum comes across the dusty carpark, valiantly carrying a massive bag. She is by far the fastest packer in the world. 'Do you think he's in there?' she mutters. I know exactly who she's referring to.

'Yep, I think he's lying there going "Why did I tell those crazy women my giant secret?" and waiting for us to go.'

'Should we say something?'

'Oh Mum. I have got absolutely no idea.'

'We could talk to the police, or we could talk to the organisers.'

'Should we?'

'But he might turn himself in. What if he does?' Mum's obviously been on the horns of this dilemma for half the night.

'Did you sleep?' I ask.

'No. Did you?'

'No. A bit towards dawn.'

'What if he's not just a son who snapped one day? What if he gets married to some poor woman? What if he's a serial murderer?'

'He trusted us. We gave him room to make his own decision. He has to live with this murder forever. If he starts making better decisions from today, he's got a better chance of recovering and going on to be a non-harmful person.'

Mother

'Darling, I've thought of a plan. We're hot and our brains aren't working very well. What about we pack the car up, have a last cup of tea, and think about it then? We can do one thing well, or two things badly. Whether we tell someone or not, we'll still have to pack up everything, and we might as well do it before the sun is overhead.'

'Excellent plan. I usually go for a final short walk before I get in the car. We can work it out while we're walking, when we're out of earshot. Also, we really need to get you to your plane on time, whether or not we dob in Andy.'

'It's not dobbing, is it? It's saving other people!'

We start to walk back to our camp, feeling the dust and the heat. A crow flies overhead, cawing.

There's a bit of packing still to do. It's exhausting packing, especially when it involves taking down a large tent and squashing the air out of the airbed, as well as finding my respectable clothes to wear on the plane — no flamboyant golden skirts in Respectability Land. And there's finding the lid of the face cream, shoving everything in a bag, wondering if I'll bother looking for the other red sock, deciding a sock here or there doesn't matter, sitting on my hairbrush accidentally. And my hives are itchy — where's the antihistamine? Botheration, as Granny used to say. It's enough to make a monkey bite its mother.

Daughter

And that's the last of it, and thank fuck. I slam the bloody boot door down on the poking-out cardboard box, hoping the boot will shut all the way. It does, and the box jolts backwards inside the car, pressing into the assorted camping crap. A little puff of dust comes off the rear bumper. I'm sweaty and I need to pee. I look around and there is no one in the carpark, so I cross over the carpark, past the cars and into a bit of scrub. I find a nice peppercorn tree and crouch down to pee, pulling my shorts out in a well-practised motion at the last minute. Looking out over the bark and through the scrub, I let the thought sink in that we are about to leave. I feel almost like I'd rather live out here with the clean air and the mates for 360 days a year and be in town for five, instead of it being the other way around. I always think this, every time I come away. But then I always wonder what I'd eat and how I'd arrange for 360 days of buddies, and reflect that we are on holiday time and everyone is on their best behaviour, and if it became the norm, the petty trivialities of life would pile up again and I'd be right back among all the dramas I've come out here to avoid.

I straighten up and hoist up my shorts. OK. What else. Mum and I made tea before we packed up our stove, so I'd better go back and have one last cuppa on the stump. There's probably not the opportunity to say goodbye to everyone, there never is, but we will have a walk around. Yes, I've got the keys in my pocket. The car has fuel. We can have a stop at Deniliquin, and I'll take Mum down to the Edwards River and show her the best paddling spot. Then lunch in Bendigo, but we can take the bypass if we're running late, and will come out close to the airport to drop Mum off. The car could probably use a wash sometime tomorrow. I should probably change into slightly more respectable clothes at some point ... or not. And it's always a good idea to go into a loo with a mirror pretty early on the trip back, because sometimes the ingrained dirt can make odd patches on your face, and you don't know why people are looking at you funny.

Oh, and I have to work out whether to inform on a murderer.

There is that.

I can't think about that right now. My brain threw up a protective shield around it while I packed. The shield was made out of itemising and grumping and checking and now it's on, it won't turn off. Perhaps Mum will have some bright idea. Perhaps he'll come out of his tent and we can talk it over.

We don't even know his last name.

I stride on back to camp, where Mum is sitting on the stump, swinging her legs and not looking particularly bothered.

'Mum!'

'Oh, hello darling!'

'Last cup of tea!'

I sit on the stump next to her and take my mug from behind us. The tea is still relatively hot, and we sit for a minute, listening to the birds and the constant conversation of the trees against the sky. Even if we are murder accomplices and our morals are lacking, I'm glad Mum came and that we had some time together. We've spent so much time in the bush when I was growing up, and now to bring her all the way out here, it feels like my idea of home has expanded. There's a companionable silence, and we cradle our hot mugs in our hands and gaze out at the scrub.

Little Onyx runs past with her brother. Mum tenses slightly. Then she relaxes.

Mother

We're having our last walk, along the sunny, winding dusty path between the gum trees, with the empty spaces that only a couple of hours go were full of tents and action and laughter. It feels like I feel: gloomy and a bit lost. Andy's tent has been looking at me all morning, accusingly, gloweringly. It's mad to feel guilty because of something you didn't do, but could we have done more? Somehow? Discussed more, been so understanding that he didn't murder his father?

It's been all the more uncomfortable because Chris and I can't mention it, owing to Andy being in his tent five metres away. Our conversation this morning has been limited to a stilted, 'Is this your hand lotion?' 'Do you want to keep this bit of celery?' Now we are away from him, walking through the bush, but there doesn't seem to be anything to say.

We return to the campsite to pick up our last things, and Andy's door is flapping open.

'He's gone now', I say. His bladder must have got the better of him. Darling, I think we can let him go.'

'Really? Do you think so? But why?'

'Chris', I say, 'I just can't dob. I can't. You have very good arguments and they're better than mine, and I think you're a better citizen than I am, but it's a gut feeling. What will Grandpa say to me at the pearly gates if I dob on anyone?'

Daughter

'OK,' I say. OK. We head back to the car, having made our decision.

'Are you sure?' I ask, slipping the key into the ignition.

'Yes, darling. Where did I put my ... oh, here it is.'

She seems pretty sure.

Light hits the windscreen of the car and comes to an abrupt halt in all the dust and grime. The car is full to the gunwales with assorted shit and there's only one CD. We're well prepared for our road trip home.

The doors clang shut and I ease the car backwards out of its spot. The peppercorn leaves wave in the early breeze and the tiny brick cottage sits sweetly by the river. I drive at a pace where I can't see a dust plume in the rear view mirror. We go past the placid green ears of saltbush and the spines of low bushes. I like driving on dirt, it reminds me of when I used to do it for a living. A white cloud or two lines the northern sky and two crows fly past us, cawing.

At least they're not going to eat Henry. He's gone in an ambulance. Perhaps I shouldn't think about that. So anyway we hit the raised road out of camp and pass a dispirited clump of people at the front tent. There are backpackers looking for a ride home, but we pass them by apologetically. We have no more room.

The car moves off, slowly. I take one last, longing look at the campsite, knowing that although there are other festivals to come, this will be the last time I am here for a long, long year. It will have to see me through all the grey, and the fluorescent lights, and the office air and the drabness of a Melbourne winter. I feel the warmth of today soaking into my skin.

'Are you sure you're sure?' I ask, rooting behind the seat for my secret stash of jerky.

'Yes, darling.'

'OK, well, bye bye camp!'

We nudge out of the carpark and pass the woolshed and brick hut where most of the infrastructure will be stored until next year. There are people who will stay and pack down everything — disassemble the marquees, unhook the soap from the taps, loop the ropes, bring down the lavatories, fill in the long drops with dirt and collect all the lost property to be taken back to Melbourne. Round up all the trolleys. Pick up endless litter and put it in bags. A myriad of jobs. I'm sad to miss the packup, it's when all the lightweights leave and only the fully committed, crazy festival heads remain and you get licence to do proper festival things that are now banned in the atmosphere of safety and beige tedium that envelops mass events nowadays. You can have a proper hot tub. The market shuts, and everyone condenses to the Arts Beach. In the evening there are guitars and singalongs and hot tubs that are properly hot, under the stars. And communal food, and good conversations with dear friends, while folding tarps and stacking books from the communal library.

I wish them all well, and hope the kitchen staff don't get too burnt out, but I know that every festival I've ever been to, the kitchen staff have gotten burnt out, and that this one is unlikely to be the exception.

And someone died! And someone died.

There's a new setup near the gate, where some people have got a voluntary drug testing marquee so that people can avoid getting charged and fined for drug driving. I'd almost say from the vibe that they're trying to signal nonverbally that there's a drug test on both roads out, but I can't be sure. Neither of us have had any drugs, so we're not bothered. I have a moment of worry about the buddies, though.

We wind our way out of the property, looking back at the line of river red gums that mark the banks of the Edwards River, and reaching from horizon to horizon. We were in there among those trees, just a minute ago. We go out through the internal fences, past the welcome gate and then out the main gate of the property. Here we go. Back to civilisation. I pull over so that Mum can drive. It's the easiest bit of highway, and who wouldn't want to drive through such beautiful country?

I'm unaccustomed to sitting in the passenger seat, and it's great having another driver. We start to mull over the events of the festival. I tell Mum how much I struggle with going back to the mainstream world, every time. She tells me that it's like going back to town after being at the beach for a couple of months. She says she can always smell the nastiness of the air when she goes back, even though it's only Hobart, one of the smallest and cleanest cities in the world.

There's a cop up ahead, waving us down. Uh oh, it looks like Mum's about to get drug tested. 'This'll be something to tell your friends,' I say.

Mum winds down the window. I'd be lying if I didn't admit that a tiny part of me is expecting the man to say, 'We have reason to believe you know the identity of the HipHaven murderer, and you're not coming forward with that information.'

'Good morning, madam,' says the squeaky clean, brawny young man.

'Hello!' says Mum, smiling and sounding highly chirpy. The poor man is about to waste a drug kit on someone whose last illicit use of narcotics was in the Hindu Kush in 1971.

Mother

There's nothing like the enjoyment of being tested for something when you know you're innocent. I turn to the young man, who looks about thirteen. This is fun.

'I've never been tested for drugs. My friends won't believe me.' He rolls his eyes a bit, but shows me the drink tester. Last time I did this I had to blow into a bag, but now you just have to count to five at it. The wonders of modern science. The drug one involves scraping your tongue. I pity the person who has to read it.

They are both, of course, 0.00, and Constable Thirteen lets me go. Another new experience. When I was young I thought Mum and Dad knew everything, and the learning curve of life would flatten out once I got to, say, my forties. Instead it's just getting steeper. I warn Chris what to expect. We keep on trying to be normal. Chris suggests we go the other way home, for a change — tiny bit longer, but different. Well, why not.

Daughter

It's hard not to comment constantly on the scenery. It's just so beautiful all the time. The silence about Andy hangs heavily between us in the car and it is squatting in such a large amount of space in my mind that I can only think of the most banal other things to say. Look at that cloud. The gum trees are different here. Is that a raven or a crow? Don't talk about Andy. Don't talk about murder. Don't start a conversation on what would ever lead you to patricide. Patricide. What a weird word.

'Right hand turn coming up ahead, Mum.'

There is only one right hand turn in the whole 100 km that she is driving for, but it is one moment of relief in the silence. I reach awkwardly behind Mum's seat for some jerky and hope the smell isn't too irritating for her.

Mother

After an hour we arrive at the first town. It's got a pub, a shop, a petrol station, small police station, a tiny school and a few scattered houses. It takes about two seconds to drive through, even keeping to the speed limit.

There's a car outside the police station. As we drive past, I see Andy at the door.

'Chris!' I exclaim. 'That was Andy, going into the police station!'

'Slow down!' she shouts, craning her neck to see.

I pull over and stop. I'm too shocked to drive on. 'Should we do anything?' I ask

'Is he going to confess?' says Chris.

'I can't think what else he'd be doing, going into a police station', I say sadly. I start the car, and we drive off.

Daughter

I feel the heartbreak feeling that often comes when you watch your mum lug a whole lot of luggage through the doors of the airport. I don't want her to go. She turns and waves with the two fingers that aren't carrying bags. I scan the bits of the car I can see for her things, for the nineteenth time. She seems to have everything. I can't believe, again, that she trusted me enough to take her to the middle of nowhere and camp in the dust with hippies. I send hopes after her; that the flight is safe, that she doesn't strain herself, that she isn't too worried.

The car pulls out into traffic on its own and a hollow feeling fills my chest and I know it will take a little while for it to go.

Mother

A few days later I'm sitting by the fire with a cup of tea reading the newspaper. And there it is, a small headline: 'Murder suspect arrested at mainland festival'. I feel horrible. Horrible for Andy, horrible for the festival, horrible for Henry. How can anything as positive, as tolerant and kind and exuberant as HipHaven become the scene for murder?

'That poor young man I told you about, the one who killed his father, has been arrested', I say sadly to James.

'What did you expect?' he asks, not very interested.

On the other hand, my friends are fascinated. 'You've never seen to many penises, Fran,' I say when I see her. 'They're all so different!' We collapse with laughter. My friends all collapse with laughter when I get on to the penises. At least the female ones do. The male ones are a bit affronted. I think they'd prefer us to gaze in awe.

'How was it?' she asks. 'Apart from the anatomy?'

'Unbelievable', I say. I tell her how hippies have changed. Now they're middle-class and polite, but the values of the hippies we used to be are still the same — the tolerance, the harmony, the workshops, the hash. She comments on

138

the photo of me that Chris put on facebook, when I was wearing wings and bathed in sunshine, surrounded by dust and scrub.

'Oh yes,' I say, pulling her scarf out of my bag, a river of gold. 'Before I forget. Thank you.' I hand it to her.

'Keep it', she says matter of factly. 'It suits you, now.'

Also published by EER

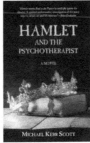
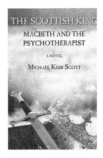

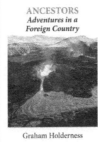

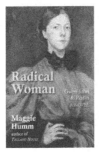

www.eerpublishing.com